PENGUIN BOOKS

FOE

J. M. Coetzee was born in Cape Town, South Africa, in 1940 and educated in South Africa and the United States. His first work of fiction was *Dusklands* (1974). This was followed by *In the Heart of the Country* (1977), which won the premier South African literary award, the CNA Prize, *Waiting for the Barbarians* (1980), which was awarded the CNA Prize, the Geoffrey Faber Memorial Prize and the James Tait Black Memorial Prize, *Life & Times of Michael K* (1983), which won the 1983 Booker Prize and the 1985 Prix Etranger Femina, *Foe* (1986), *White Writing* (1988), a collection of essays and *Age of Iron* (1990) which won the 1990 *Sunday Express* Book of the Year Award. J. M. Coetzee was winner of the Jerusalem Prize for 1987. Many of his books are published by Penguin. His other works include translations, linguistic studies and literary criticism. He is at present Professor of General Literature at the University of Cape Town. All of his novels have received the highest critical acclaim; writing for the *Sunday Times*, Victoria Glendinning said, 'It is hard to convey . . . just what Coetzee's special quality is. His writing gives off whiffs of Conrad, of Nabokov, of Golding, of the Paul Theroux of *The Mosquito Coast*.' And Bernard Levin has described him as 'an artist of weight and depth that put him in a category beyond ordinary comparison'.

J. M. COETZEE

FOE

PENGUIN BOOKS

PENGUIN BOOKS

Published by the Penguin Group
Penguin Books Ltd, 27 Wrights Lane, London W8 5TZ, England
Penguin Books USA Inc., 375 Hudson Street, New York, New York 10014, USA
Penguin Books Australia Ltd, Ringwood, Victoria, Australia
Penguin Books Canada Ltd, 10 Alcorn Avenue, Toronto, Ontario, Canada M4V 3B2
Penguin Books (NZ) Ltd, 182–190 Wairau Road, Auckland 10, New Zealand

Penguin Books Ltd, Registered Offices: Harmondsworth, Middlesex, England

First published in Great Britain by Martin Secker & Warburg Ltd, 1986
First published in the USA by Viking 1987
Published in Penguin Books 1987
9 10 8

Printed in England by Clays Ltd, St Ives plc

I

'*A*t last I could row no further. My hands were blistered, my back was burned, my body ached. With a sigh, making barely a splash, I slipped overboard. With slow strokes, my long hair floating about me, like a flower of the sea, like an anemone, like a jellyfish of the kind you see in the waters of Brazil, I swam towards the strange island, for a while swimming as I had rowed, against the current, then all at once free of its grip, carried by the waves into the bay and on to the beach.

'There I lay sprawled on the hot sand, my head filled with the orange blaze of the sun, my petticoat (which was all I had escaped with) baking dry upon me, tired, grateful, like all the saved.

'A dark shadow fell upon me, not of a cloud but of a man with a dazzling halo about him. "Castaway," I said with my thick dry tongue. "I am cast away. I am all alone." And I held out my sore hands.

'The man squatted down beside me. He was black: a Negro with a head of fuzzy wool, naked save for a pair of rough drawers. I lifted myself and studied the flat face, the small dull eyes, the broad nose, the thick lips, the skin not black but a dark grey, dry as if coated with dust. *"Agua,"* I said, trying Portuguese, and made a sign of drinking. He gave no reply, but regarded me as he would a seal or a porpoise thrown up by the waves, that would shortly expire and might then be cut up for food. At his side he had a spear. I have come to the wrong island, I thought, and let my head sink: I have come to an island of cannibals.

'He reached out and with the back of his hand touched my arm. He is trying my flesh, I thought. But by and by my breathing slowed and I grew calmer. He smelled of fish, and of sheepswool on a hot day.

'Then, since we could not stay thus forever, I sat up and again began to make motions of drinking. I had rowed all morning, I had not drunk since the night before, I no longer cared if he killed me afterwards so long as I had water.

'The Negro rose and signed me to follow. He led me, stiff and sore, across sand-dunes and along a path ascending to the hilly interior of the island. But we had scarcely begun to climb when I felt a sharp hurt, and drew from my heel a long black-tipped thorn. Though I chafed it, the heel quickly swelled till I could not so much as hobble for the pain. The Negro offered me his back, indicating he would carry me. I hesitated to accept, for he was a slight fellow, shorter than I. But there was no help for it. So part-way skipping on one leg, part-way riding on his back, with my petticoat gathered up and my chin brushing his springy hair, I ascended the hillside, my fear of him abating in this strange backwards embrace. He took no heed where he set his feet, I noted, but crushed under his soles whole clusters of the thorns that had pierced my skin.

'For readers reared on travellers' tales, the words *desert isle* may conjure up a place of soft sands and shady trees where brooks run to quench the castaway's thirst and ripe fruit falls into his hand, where no more is asked of him than to drowse the days away till a ship calls to fetch him home. But the island on which I was cast away was quite another place: a great rocky hill with a flat top, rising sharply from the sea on all sides except one, dotted with drab bushes that never flowered and never shed their leaves. Off the island grew beds of brown seaweed which, borne ashore by the waves, gave off a noisome stench and supported swarms of large pale fleas. There were ants scurrying everywhere, of the same kind we had in Bahia, and another pest, too, living in the dunes: a tiny insect that hid between your toes and ate its way into the flesh. Even Friday's hard skin was not proof against it: there were bleeding cracks in his feet, though he paid them no heed. I saw no snakes, but lizards came out in the heat of the day to sun themselves, some small and agile, others large and clumsy, with blue ruffs about their gills which they would flare out when alarmed, and hiss, and glare. I caught one of them in a bag' and tried to tame it, feeding it flies; but it would not take dead meat, so at last I set it free. Also there were apes (of whom I will say more later) and birds, birds everywhere: not only flocks of sparrows (or so I called them) that flitted all day chirruping from bush to bush, but on the cliffs above the sea great tribes of gulls and mews and gannets and cormorants, so that the rocks were white with their droppings. And in the sea porpoises and seals and fish of all kinds. So if the company of brutes had been enough for me, I might have lived most happily on my island. But who, accustomed to the fullness of human speech, can be content with caws and chirps and screeches, and the barking of seals, and the moan of the wind?]

'At last we came to the end of our climb and my porter halted to catch his breath. I found myself on a level plateau not far from some kind of encampment. On all sides stretched the shimmering sea, while to the east the ship that had brought me receded under full sail.

'My one thought was for water. I did not care to what fate I was being borne so long as I could drink. At the gate of the encampment stood a man, dark-skinned and heavily bearded. "*Agua,*" I said, making signs. He gestured to the Negro, and I saw I was talking to a European. "*Fala inglez?*" I asked, as I had learned to say in Brazil. He nodded. The Negro brought me a bowl of water. I drank, and he brought more. It was the best water I ever had.

'The stranger's eyes were green, his hair burnt to a straw colour. I judged he was sixty years of age. He wore (let me give my description of him all together) a jerkin, and drawers to below his knees, such as we see watermen wear on the Thames, and a tall cap rising in a cone, all of these made of pelts laced together, the fur outwards, and a stout pair of sandals. In his belt were a short stick and a knife. A mutineer, was my first thought: yet another mutineer, set ashore by a merciful captain, with one of the Negroes of the island,

8

whom he has made his servant. "My name is Susan Barton," I said. "I was cast adrift by the crew of the ship yonder. They killed their master and did this to me." And all at once, though I had remained dry-eyed through all the insults done me on board ship and through the hours of despair when I was alone on the waves with the captain lying dead at my feet, a handspike jutting from his eye-socket, I fell to crying. I sat on the bare earth with my sore foot between my hands and rocked back and forth and sobbed like a child, while the stranger (who was of course the Cruso I told you of) gazed at me more as if I were a fish cast up by the waves than an unfortunate fellow-creature.

'I have told you how Cruso was dressed; now let me tell you of his habitation.

'In the centre of the flat hilltop was a cluster of rocks as high as a house. In the angle between two of these rocks Cruso had built himself a hut of poles and reeds, the reeds artfully thatched together and woven in and out of the poles with fronds to form roof and walls. A fence, with a gate that turned on leather hinges, completed an encampment in the shape of a triangle which Cruso termed his castle. Within the fence, protected from the apes, grew a patch of wild bitter lettuce. This lettuce, with fish and birds' eggs, formed our sole diet on the island, as you shall hear.

'In the hut Cruso had a narrow bed, which was all his furniture. The bare earth formed the floor. For his bed Friday had a mat under the eaves.

'Drying my tears at last, I asked Cruso for a needle or some such instrument to remove the thorn from my foot. He brought out a needle made of a fishbone with a hole pierced through the broad end, by what means I do not know, and watched in silence while I took out the thorn.

→ '"Let me tell you my story," said I; "for I am sure you are wondering who I am and how I come to be here.

'"My name is Susan Barton, and I am a woman alone. My father was a Frenchman who fled to England to escape the persecutions in Flanders. His name was properly Berton, but, as happens, it became corrupted in the mouths of strangers. My mother was an Englishwoman.

'"Two years ago my only daughter was abducted and conveyed to the New World by an Englishman, a factor and agent in the carrying trade. I followed in search of her. Arriving in Bahia, I was met with denials and, when I persisted, with rudeness and threats. The officers of the Crown afforded me no aid, saying it was a matter between the English. I lived in lodgings, and took in sewing, and searched, and waited, but saw no trace of my child. So, despairing at last, and my means giving out, I embarked for Lisbon on a merchantman.

'"Ten days out from port, as if my misfortunes were not great enough, the crew mutinied. Bursting into their captain's cabin, they slew him heartlessly even while he pleaded for his life. Those of their fellows who were not with them they clapped in irons. They put me in a boat with the captain's corpse beside me, and set us adrift. Why they chose to cast me away I do not know. But those whom we have abused we customarily grow to hate, and wish never to lay eyes on

again. The heart of man is a dark forest – that is one
of the sayings they have in Brazil.

'"As chance would have it – or perhaps the mutiny
had been so ordered – I was set adrift in sight of this
island. *'Remos!'* shouted the seaman from the deck,
meaning I should take up the oars and row. But I was
shaking with terror. So while they laughed and jeered
I drifted hither and thither on the waves, till the wind
came up.

'"All morning, while the ship drew away (I believe
the mutineers were of a mind to become pirates off
Hispaniola), I rowed with the dead captain at my feet.
My palms were soon blistered – see! – but I dared not
rest, fearing that the current would draw me past your
island. Worse by far than the pain of rowing was the
prospect of being adrift at night in the vast emptiness
of the sea, when, as I have heard, the monsters of the
deep ascend in quest of prey.

'"Then at last I could row no further. My hands
were raw, my back was burned, my body ached. With
a sigh, making barely a splash, I slipped overboard
and began to swim towards your island. The waves
took me and bore me on to the beach. The rest you
know."

'With these words I presented myself to Robinson
Cruso, in the days when he still ruled over his island,
and became his second subject, the first being his
manservant Friday.

'I would gladly now recount to you the history of
this singular Cruso, as I heard it from his own lips.
But the stories he told me were so various, and so
hard to reconcile one with another, that I was more

and more driven to conclude age and isolation had taken their toll on his memory, and he no longer knew for sure what was truth, what fancy. Thus one day he would say his father had been a wealthy merchant whose counting-house he had quit in search of adventure. But the next day he would tell me he had been a poor lad of no family who had shipped as a cabin-boy and been captured by the Moors (he bore a scar on his arm which was, he said, the mark of the branding-iron) and escaped and made his way to the New World. Sometimes he would say he had dwelt on his island the past fifteen years, he and Friday, none but they having been spared when their ship went down. "Was Friday then a child, when the ship went down?" I asked. "Aye, a child, a mere child, a little slave-boy," replied Cruso. Yet at other times, as for instance when he was in the grip of the fever (and should we not believe that in fever as in drunkenness the truth speaks itself willy-nilly?) he would tell stories of cannibals, of how Friday was a cannibal whom he had saved from being roasted and devoured by fellow-cannibals. "Might the cannibals not return to reclaim Friday?" I would ask, and he would nod. "Is that why you are forever looking out to sea: to be warned of the return of the cannibals?" I would pursue; and he would nod again. So in the end I did not know what was truth, what was lies, and what was mere rambling.

'But let me return to my relation.

'Tired to the bone, I asked to lie down, and fell at once into a deep sleep. The sun was sinking when I awoke, and Friday was preparing our supper. Though it was no more than fish roasted over coals and served with lettuce, I ate with gusto. Grateful to have my belly full and my feet on solid earth again, I expressed my thanks to this singular saviour of mine. I would have told him more about myself too, about my quest for my stolen daughter, about the mutiny. But he asked nothing, gazing out instead into the setting sun, nodding to himself as though a voice spoke privately inside him that he was listening to.

'"May I ask, sir," said I, after a while: "Why in all these years have you not built a boat and made your escape from this island?"

'"And where should I escape to?" he replied, smiling to himself as though no answer were possible.

'"Why, you might sail to the coast of Brazil, or meet a ship and be saved."

'"Brazil is hundreds of miles distant, and full of cannibals," said he. "As for sailing-ships, we shall see sailing-ships as well and better by staying at home."

'"I beg to disagree," said I. "I spent two long years in Brazil and met no cannibals there."

'"You were in Bahia," said he. "Bahia is naught but an island on the rim of the Brazilian forests."

'So I early began to see it was a waste of breath to urge Cruso to save himself. Growing old on his island kingdom with no one to say him nay had so narrowed his horizon – when the horizon all around us was so vast and so majestic! – that he had come to be persuaded he knew all there was to know about the world. Besides, as I later found, the desire to escape had dwindled within him. His heart was set on remaining to his dying day king of his tiny realm. In truth it was not fear of pirates or cannibals that held him from making bonfires or dancing about on the hilltop waving his hat, but indifference to salvation, and habit, and the stubbornness of old age.

'It was time to retire. Cruso offered to give up his bed, but I would not accept, preferring to have Friday spread me a bed of grass on the floor. There I laid myself down, an arm's-length from Cruso (for the hut was small). Last night I had been bound for home; tonight I was a castaway. Long hours I lay awake, unable to believe the change in my fortunes, troubled too by the pain of my blistered hands. Then I fell asleep. I awoke once in the night. The wind had dropped; I could hear the singing of crickets and, far away, the roar of the waves. "I am safe, I am on an island, all will be well," I whispered to myself, and hugged myself tight, and slept again.

'I was woken by the drumming of rain on the roof. It was morning; Friday was crouched before the stove (I have not yet told you of Cruso's stove, which was built very neatly of stone), feeding the fire, blowing it into life. At first I was ashamed that he should see me abed, but then I reminded myself of how free the ladies of Bahia were before their servants, and so felt better. Cruso came in, and we breakfasted well on birds' eggs, while the rain dripped here and there through the roof and hissed on the hot stones. In time the rain ceased and the sun came out, drawing wisps of steam from the earth, and the wind resumed and blew without respite till the next lull and the next rain. Wind, rain, wind, rain: such was the pattern of the days in that place, and had been, for all I knew, since the beginning of time. If one circumstance above all determined me to escape, whatever the cost, it was not the loneliness nor the rudeness of the life, nor the monotony of the diet, but the wind that day after day whistled in my ears and tugged at my hair and blew sand into my eyes, till sometimes I would kneel in a corner of the hut with my head in my arms and moan to myself, on and on, to hear some other sound than the beating of the wind; or later, when I had taken to bathing in the sea, would hold my breath and dip my head under the water merely to know what it was to have silence. Very likely you will say to yourself: In Patagonia the wind blows all year without let, and the Patagonians do not hide their heads, so why does she? But the Patagonians, knowing no home but Patagonia, have no reason to doubt that the wind blows at all seasons without let in all quarters of the globe; whereas I know better.

'Before setting out to perform his island duties, Cruso gave me his knife and warned me not to venture from his castle; for the apes, he said, would not be as wary of a woman as they were of him and Friday. I wondered at this: was a woman, to an ape, a different species from a man? Nevertheless, I prudently obeyed, and stayed at home, and rested.

'Save for the knife, all tools on the island were of wood or stone. The spade with which Cruso levelled his terraces (I shall have more to say of the terraces later) was a narrow wooden thing with a crooked handle, carved all of a piece and hardened in the fire. His mattock was a sharp stone lashed to a stick. The bowls we ate and drank from were crude blocks of wood hollowed out by scraping and burning. For there was no clay on the island to mould and bake, and such trees as there were were puny, stunted by the wind, their twisted stems seldom broader than my hand. It seemed a great pity that from the wreck Cruso should have brought away no more than a knife. For had he rescued even the simplest of carpenter's tools, and some spikes and bars and suchlike, he might have fashioned better tools, and with better tools contrived a less laborious life, or even built a boat and escaped to civilization.

'In the hut there was nothing but the bed, which was made of poles bound together with thongs, crude in workmanship yet sturdy, and in a corner a pile of cured apeskins, that made the hut smell like a tanner's storehouse (in time I grew used to the smell, and missed it after I had put the island behind me; even today when I smell new leather I grow drowsy), and the stove, in which the embers of the last fire were always left banked, for making new fire was tedious work.

'What I chiefly hoped to find was not there. Cruso kept no journal, perhaps because he lacked paper and ink, but more likely, I now believe, because he lacked the inclination to keep one, or, if he ever possessed the inclination, had lost it. I searched the poles that supported the roof, and the legs of the bed, but found no carvings, not even notches to indicate that he counted the years of his banishment or the cycles of the moon.

'Later, when I had grown freer with him, I told

him of my surprise. "Suppose," said I, "that one day we are saved. Would you not regret it that you could not bring back with you some record of your years of shipwreck, so that what you have passed through shall not die from memory? And if we are never saved, but perish one by one, as may happen, would you not wish for a memorial to be left behind, so that the next voyagers to make landfall here, whoever they may be, may read and learn about us, and perhaps shed a tear? For surely, with every day that passes, our memories grow less certain, as even a statue in marble is worn away by rain, till at last we can no longer tell what shape the sculptor's hand gave it. What memories do you even now preserve of the fatal storm, the prayers of your companions, your terror when the waves engulfed you, your gratitude as you were cast up on the shore, your first stumbling explorations, your fear of savage beasts, the discomforts of those first nights (did you not tell me you slept in a tree?)? Is it not possible to manufacture paper and ink and set down what traces remain of these memories, so that they will outlive you; or, failing paper and ink, to burn the story upon wood, or engrave it upon rock? We may lack many things on this island, but certainly time is not one of them."

'I spoke fervently, I believe, but Cruso was unmoved. "Nothing is forgotten," said he; and then: "Nothing I have forgotten is worth the re-membering."

'"You are mistaken!" I cried. "I do not wish to dispute, but you have forgotten much, and with every day that passes you forget more! There is no shame in forgetting: it is our nature to forget as it is our nature to grow old and pass away. But seen from too remote a vantage, life begins to lose its particularity. All shipwrecks become the same shipwreck, all castaways the same castaway, sunburnt, lonely, clad in the skins of the beasts he has slain. The truth that makes your story yours alone, that sets you apart from the old mariner by the fireside spinning yarns of sea-monsters and mermaids, resides in a thousand touches which today may seem of no importance, such as: When you made your needle (the needle you store in your belt), by what means did you pierce the eye? When you sewed your hat, what did you use for thread? Touches like these will one day persuade your countrymen that it is all true, every word, there was indeed once an island in the middle of the ocean where the wind blew and the gulls cried from the cliffs and a man named Cruso paced about in his apeskin clothes, scanning the horizon for a sail.''

'Cruso's great head of tawny hair and his beard that was never cut glowed in the dying light. He opened and closed his hands, sinewy, rough-skinned hands, toil-hardened.

"There is the bile of seabirds," I urged. "There are cuttlefish bones. There are gulls' quills."

'Cruso raised his head and cast me a look full of defiance. "I will leave behind my terraces and walls," he said. "They will be enough. They will be more than enough." And he fell silent again. As for myself, I wondered who would cross the ocean to see terraces and walls, of which we surely had an abundance at home; but I held my peace.]

'We continued to sleep in the hut together, he and I, he on his bed, I on the bed of grass Friday laid for me and changed every third day, very thick and comfortable. When the nights grew cold I would draw a cover of skins over me, for all this time I had no more clothes than the petticoat I had come ashore in ; but I preferred not to have the skins upon me, for to my nostrils their smell was still very strong.

'Sometimes Cruso kept me awake with the sounds he made in his sleep, chiefly the grinding of his teeth. For so far had his teeth decayed that it had grown a habit with him to grind them together constantly, those that were left, to still the ache. Indeed, it was no pretty sight to see him take his food in his unwashed hands and gnaw at it on the left side, where it hurt him less. But Bahia, and the life I had lived there, had taught me not to be dainty.

'I dreamed of the murdered ship's-master. In my dream I saw him floating southward in his puny boat with the oars crossed on his breast and the ugly spike sticking out of his eye. The sea was tossed with huge waves, the wind howled, the rain beat down; yet the boat did not sink, but drifted slowly on toward the province of the iceberg, and would drift there, it seemed to me, caked in ice, till the day of our resurrection. He was a kindly man – let me say so now, lest I forget – who deserved a better end.

'Cruso's warning against the apes made me chary of leaving the encampment. Nevertheless, on the third day of my marooning, after Cruso and Friday had gone off to their labours, I ventured out and searched the descent till I found the path up which Friday had borne me, and followed it down to the shore, watching where I trod, for I still had no shoes. I roamed along the beach awhile, keeping an eye out to sea, though it seemed early yet for rescue to come. I waded in the water, amused by the gay-coloured little fish that stopped to nibble my toes and taste what kind of creature I was. Cruso's island is no bad place to be cast away, I thought, if one must be cast away. Then about noon I climbed the slope and set about collecting firewood, as I had undertaken to do, mightily pleased with my excursion.

'When Cruso returned he knew at once I had been exploring, and burst out in a passion. "While you live under my roof you will do as I instruct!" he cried, striking his spade into the earth, not even waiting till Friday was out of earshot. But if he thought by angry looks to inspire me to fear and slavish obedience, he soon found he was mistaken. "I am on your island, Mr Cruso, not by choice but by ill luck," I replied, standing up (and I was nearly as tall as he). "I am a castaway, not a prisoner. If I had shoes, or if you would give me the means to make shoes, I would not need to steal about like a thief."

'Later in the day, when my temper had cooled, I asked Cruso's pardon for these tart words, and he seemed to forgive me, though grudgingly. Then I asked again for a needle and gut, to make myself shoes. To which he replied that shoes were not made in a twinkle, like handkerchiefs, that he would himself make me shoes, in due time. Days passed, however, and still I was without shoes.

'I asked Cruso about the apes. When he first arrived,

he said, they had roamed all over the island, bold and mischievous. He had killed many, after which the remainder had retreated to the cliffs of what he called the North Bluff. On my walks I sometimes heard their cries and saw them leaping from rock to rock. In size they were between a cat and a fox, grey, with black faces and black paws. I saw no harm in them; but Cruso held them a pest, and he and Friday killed them whenever they could, with clubs, and skinned them, and cured their pelts, and sewed them together to make clothes and blankets and suchlike.

'One evening, as I was preparing our supper, my hands being full, I turned to Friday and said, "Bring more wood, Friday." Friday heard me, I could have sworn, but he did not stir. So I said the word "Wood" again, indicating the fire; upon which he stood up, but did no more. Then Cruso spoke. "Firewood, Friday," he said; and Friday went off and fetched wood from the woodpile.

'My first thought was that Friday was like a dog that heeds but one master; yet it was not so. "*Firewood* is the word I have taught him," said Cruso. "*Wood* he does not know." I found it strange that Friday should not understand that firewood was a kind of wood, as pinewood is a kind of wood, or poplarwood; but I let it pass. Not till after we had eaten, when we were sitting watching the stars, as had grown to be our habit, did I speak again.

'"How many words of English does Friday know?" I asked.

'"As many as he needs," replied Cruso. "This is not England, we have no need of a great stock of words."

'"You speak as if language were one of the banes of life, like money or the pox," said I. "Yet would it not have lightened your solitude had Friday been master of English? You and he might have experienced, all these years, the pleasures of conversation; you might have brought home to him some of the blessings of civilization and made him a better man. What benefit is there in a life of silence?"

'To this Cruso gave no reply, but instead beckoned Friday nearer. "Sing, Friday," he said. "Sing for Mistress Barton."

'Whereupon Friday raised his face to the stars, closed his eyes, and, obedient to his master, began to hum in a low voice. I listened but could make out no tune. Cruso tapped my knee. "The voice of man," he said. I failed to understand his meaning; but he raised a finger to his lips to still me. In the dark we listened to Friday's humming.

'At last Friday paused. "Is Friday an imbecile incapable of speech?" I asked. "Is that what you mean to tell me?" (For I repeat, I found Friday in all matters a dull fellow.)

'Cruso motioned Friday nearer. "Open your mouth," he told him, and opened his own. Friday opened his mouth. "Look," said Cruso. I looked, but saw nothing in the dark save the glint of teeth white as ivory. "La-la-la," said Cruso, and motioned to Friday to repeat. "Ha-ha-ha," said Friday from the back of his throat. "He has no tongue," said Cruso. Gripping Friday by the hair, he brought his face close to mine. "Do you see?" he said. "It is too dark," said I. "La-la-la," said Cruso. "Ha-ha-ha," said Friday. I drew away, and Cruso released Friday's hair. "He has no tongue," he said. "That is why he does not speak. They cut out his tongue."

'I stared in amazement. "Who cut out his tongue?"

'"The slavers."

'"The slavers cut out his tongue and sold him into slavery? The slave-hunters of Africa? But surely he was a mere child when they took him. Why would they cut out a child's tongue?"

'Cruso gazed steadily back at me. Though I cannot now swear to it, I believe he was smiling. "Perhaps the slavers, who are Moors, hold the tongue to be a delicacy," he said. "Or perhaps they grew weary of listening to Friday's wails of grief, that went on day and night. Perhaps they wanted to prevent him from ever telling his story: who he was, where his home lay, how it came about that he was taken. Perhaps they cut out the tongue of every cannibal they took, as a punishment. How will we ever know the truth?"

'"It is a terrible story," I said. A silence fell. Friday took up our utensils and retired into the darkness. "Where is the justice in it? First a slave and now a castaway too. Robbed of his childhood and consigned to a life of silence. Was Providence sleeping?"

'"If Providence were to watch over all of us," said Cruso, "who would be left to pick the cotton and cut the sugar-cane? For the business of the world to prosper, Providence must sometimes wake and sometimes sleep, as lower creatures do." He saw I shook my head, so went on. "You think I mock Providence. But perhaps it is the doing of Providence that Friday finds himself on an island under a lenient master, rather than in Brazil, under the planter's lash, or in Africa, where the forests teem with cannibals. Perhaps it is for the best, though we do not see it so, that he should be here, and that I should be here, and now that you should be here."

'Hitherto I had found Friday a shadowy creature and paid him little more attention than I would have given any house-slave in Brazil. But now I began to look on him – I could not help myself – with the horror we reserve for the mutilated. It was no comfort that his mutilation was secret, closed behind his lips (as some other mutilations are hidden by clothing), that outwardly he was like any Negro. Indeed, it was the very secretness of his loss that caused me to shrink from him. I could not speak, while he was about, without being aware how lively were the movements of the tongue in my own mouth. I saw pictures in my mind of pincers gripping his tongue and a knife slicing into it, as must have happened, and I shuddered. I covertly observed him as he ate, and with distaste heard the tiny coughs he gave now and then to clear his throat, saw how he did his chewing between his front teeth, like a fish. I caught myself flinching when he came near, or holding my breath so as not to have to smell him. Behind his back I wiped the utensils his hands had touched. I was ashamed to behave thus, but for a time was not mistress of my own actions. Sorely I regretted that Cruso had ever told me the story.

'The next day after our conversation, when Cruso returned from his terraces, I was walking about in sandals. But if I expected thanks for the labour I had saved him, I received none. "A little patience and you would have had better shoes than that," he said. This was very likely true, for the sandals were clumsily made. Yet I could not let his words pass. "Patience has turned me into a prisoner," I retorted. Whereupon Cruso wheeled about angrily and picked up the skins from which I had cut my shoes and hurled them with all his might over the fence.

'Seeing that he was not to be mollified, I took myself off down the path to the shore, and wandered there till I came to a place where the beach was covered in seaweed that had been washed ashore, and lay rotting, and where clouds of fleas, or sand-fleas, rose at every step. There I paused, my temper cooling. He is bitter, I told myself, and why should he not be? After years of unquestioned and solitary mastery, he sees his realm invaded and has tasks set upon him by a woman. I made a vow to keep a tighter rein on my tongue. Worse fates might have befallen me than to be abandoned on an island ruled over by a countryman with the foresight to swim ashore with a knife at his belt and a slave at his side. I might as easily have been cast away alone on an island infested with lions and snakes, or on an island where rain never fell, or else on the island home of some foreign adventurer gone mad with solitude, naked, bestial, living on raw flesh.

'So I returned in a contrite spirit and went to Cruso and asked his pardon for taking the skins, and gratefully accepted the food Friday had set aside. When I lay down to sleep that night I seemed to feel the earth sway beneath me. I told myself it was a memory of the rocking of the ship coming back unbidden. But it was not so: it was the rocking of the island itself as it floated on the sea. I thought: It is a sign, a sign I am becoming an island-dweller. I am forgetting what it is to live on the mainland. I stretched out my arms and laid my palms on the earth, and, yes, the rocking persisted, the rocking of the island as it sailed through the sea and the night bearing into the future its freight of gulls and sparrows and fleas and apes and castaways, all unconscious now, save me. I fell asleep smiling. I believe it was the first time I smiled since I embarked for the New World.

'They say Britain is an island too, a great island. But that is a mere geographer's notion. The earth under our feet is firm in Britain, as it never was on Cruso's island.

'Now that I had shoes, I took to walking the shore-line every day, as far in either direction as I could. I told myself I was keeping watch for a sail. But too often my eyes would settle on the horizon in a kind of fixity till, lulled by the beating of the wind and the roar of the waves and the crunch of the sand under my feet, I would fall into a waking slumber. I found a hollow in the rocks where I could lie sheltered from the wind and gaze out to sea. In time I grew to think of this as my private retreat, the one place reserved for me on an island owned by another; though in truth the island no more belonged to Cruso than to the King of Portugal or indeed to Friday or the cannibals of Africa.

'There is more, much more, I could tell you about the life we lived: how we kept the fire smouldering day and night; how we made salt; how, lacking soap, we cleaned ourselves with ash. Once I asked Cruso whether he knew no way of fashioning a lamp or a candle so that we should not have to retire when darkness fell, like brutes. Cruso responded in the following words: "Which is easier: to learn to see in the dark, or to kill a whale and seethe it down for the sake of a candle?" There were many tart retorts I might have made; but, remembering my vow, I held my tongue. The simple truth was, Cruso would brook no change on his island.

'I had been there about a month when one morning Cruso came home from the terraces complaining he was unwell. Seeing he was shivering, I put him to bed and covered him warmly. "It is the old fever that came with me," he said. "There is no cure, it must run its course."

'For twelve days and nights I nursed him, sometimes holding him down when fits of raving overtook him, when he sobbed or beat with his fists and shouted in Portuguese at figures he saw in the shadows. One night, indeed, when for hours he had been moaning and shivering, his hands and feet cold as ice, I lay down beside him, holding him in my arms to warm him, fearing he would die otherwise. In my embrace he at last fell asleep, and I slept too, though uneasily.

'All this time Friday made no effort to help me, but on the contrary shunned the hut as though we two had the plague. At daybreak he would set off with his fishing-spear; returning, he would put his catch down beside the stove, gutted and scaled, and then retire to a far corner of the garden, where he would sleep curled on his side like a cat, or else play over and over again

on his little reed flute a tune of six notes, always the
same. This tune, of which he seemed never to tire,
grew so to annoy me that one day I marched over and
dashed the flute from his hands and would have scold-
ed him too, whether or not he understood, had I not
feared to wake Cruso. Friday sprang to his feet, his
eyes wide with surprise, for I had never lost patience
with him before, or indeed paid him much heed.

'Then Cruso began to mend. The wild glitter in his
eye abated, the lines of his face softened, his bouts of
raving ended, he slept peacefully. His appetite came
back. Soon he was walking from hut to garden
unaided, and giving Friday orders.

'I greeted his return to health with gladness. In
Brazil I had seen younger men carried off by the fever;
there had been a night and a day, indeed, when I was
sure Cruso was dying, and looked forward with
dismay to being left alone with Friday. It was the vigorous life he lived, I believe, that saved Cruso – the
vigorous life and the simple diet, not any skill of
mine.

'Shortly hereafter we had a great storm, the wind
howling and rain falling in torrents. In one of the
gusts part of the roof of the hut was torn off and the
fire we guarded so jealously drowned. We moved
the bed to the last dry corner; even there the floor
soon turned to mud.

'I had thought Friday would be terrified by the
clamour of the elements (I had never known such a
storm, and pitied the poor mariners at sea). But no,
Friday sat under the eaves with his head on his knees
and slept like a baby.

'After two nights and a day the rain abated and we came out to stretch our limbs. We found the garden near washed away, and where the path had led down the hillside a gully as deep as my waist had been cut by the waters. The beach was covered in seaweed tossed up by the waves. Then it began to rain again, and for a third night we retired to our miserable shelter, hungry, cold, unable to make fire.

'That night Cruso, who had seemed quite mended, complained of being hot, and tossed off his clothes and lay panting. Then he began to rave and throw himself from side to side as if unable to breathe, till I thought the bed would break. I gripped him by the shoulders and tried to soothe him, but he beat me away. Great tremors ran through him; he grew stiff as a board and began to bellow about *Masa* or *Massa*, a word with no meaning I can discover. Woken by the din, Friday took out his flute and began to play his damnable tune, till what with the rain and the wind and Cruso's shouting and Friday's music, I could have believed myself in a madhouse. But I continued to hold Cruso and soothe him, and at last he grew still, and Friday ceased his noise, and even the rain grew softer. I stretched myself out against Cruso to warm his body with mine; in time the trembling gave out and both he and I slept.

'I came to myself in daylight, in an unfamiliar silence, the storm having at last blown itself out. A hand was exploring my body. So befuddled was I that I thought myself still aboard the ship, in the Portuguese captain's bed. But then I turned and saw Cruso's wild hair and the great beard he never cut and his yellow eyes, and I knew it was all true, I was indeed cast away on an island with a man named Cruso, who though an Englishman was as strange to me as a Laplander. I pushed his hand away and made to rise, but he held me. No doubt I might have freed myself, for I was stronger than he. But I thought, He has not known a woman for fifteen years, why should he not have his desire? So I resisted no more but let him do as he wished. When I left the hut Friday was nowhere in sight, for which I was glad. I walked some distance, then sat down to collect myself. Around me in the bushes settled a flock of sparrows, cocking their heads curiously, quite unafraid, having known no harm from man since the beginning of time. Was I to regret what had passed between Cruso and me? Would it have been better had we continued to live as brother and sister, or host and guest, or master and servant, or whatever it was we had been? Chance had cast me on his island, chance had thrown me in his arms. In a world of chance, is there a better and a worse? We yield to a stranger's embrace or give ourselves to the waves; for the blink of an eyelid our vigilance relaxes; we are asleep; and when we awake, we have lost the direction of our lives. What are these blinks of an eyelid, against which the only defence is an eternal and inhuman wakefulness? Might they not be the cracks and chinks through which another voice, other voices, speak in our lives? By what right do we close our ears to them? The questions echoed in my head without answer.

'I was walking one day at the north end of the island, on the Bluff, when I spied Friday below me bearing on his shoulder a log or beam nearly as long as himself. While I watched, he crossed the shelf of rock that stretched out from the cliff-face, launched his log upon the water – which was deep at that place – and straddled it.

'I had often observed Friday at his fishing, which he did standing on the rocks, waiting till a fish swam below him and then darting his spear at it with great dexterity. How he could spear fish belly-down upon his clumsy vessel was not plain to me.

'But Friday was not fishing. After paddling out some hundred yards from the shelf into the thickest of the seaweed, he reached into a bag that hung about his neck and brought out handfuls of white flakes which he began to scatter over the water. At first I thought this was bait to lure the fish to him; but no, when he had strewn all his flakes he turned his log-boat about and steered it back to the ledge, where he landed it with great difficulty through the swell.

'Curious to find what he had been casting on the waves, I waited that evening till he had gone to fill the water-bowls. Then I searched under his mat and discovered a little bag with a drawstring, and turning it out found some few white petals and buds from the brambles that were at the time flowering on parts of the island. So I concluded he had been making an offering to the god of the waves to cause the fish to run plentifully, or performing some other such superstitious observance.

'The sea continuing calm the next day, I crossed the rocks below the Bluff as Friday had done till I stood at the edge of the shelf. The water was cold and dark;

when I thought of committing myself to those depths and swimming out, whether on a log or not, among the circling arms of the seaweed, where no doubt cuttlefish hung in stealth waiting for prey to swim into their grasp, I shivered. Of Friday's petals not a trace was left.

'Hitherto I had given to Friday's life as little thought as I would have a dog's or any other dumb beast's – less, indeed, for I had a horror of his mutilated state which made me shut him from my mind, and flinch away when he came near me. This casting of petals was the first sign I had that a spirit or soul – call it what you will – stirred beneath that dull and unpleasing exterior.

'"Where did the ship go down on which you and Friday sailed?" I asked Cruso.

'He indicated a part of the coast I had never visited.

'"If we could dive to the wreck, even now," I said, "we might save from it tools of the greatest utility. A saw, for instance, or an axe, both of which we lack. Timbers too we might loosen and bring back. Is there no way to explore the wreck? Might Friday not swim out to it, or float out on a log, and then dive down, with a rope tied about his middle for safety?"

'"The ship lies on the bed of the ocean, broken by the waves and covered in sand," Cruso replied. "What has survived the salt and seaworm will not be worth the saving. We have a roof over our heads, made without saw or axe. We sleep, we eat, we live. We have no need of tools."

'He spoke as if tools were heathenish inventions. Yet I knew if I had swum ashore with a saw tied to my ankle he would have taken it and used it most happily.

'Let me tell you of Cruso's terraces.

'The terraces covered much of the hillside at the eastern end of the island, where they were best sheltered from the wind. There were twelve levels of terracing at the time I arrived, each some twenty paces deep and banked with stone walls a yard thick and at their highest as high as a man's head. Within each terrace the ground was levelled and cleared; the stones that made up the walls had been dug out of the earth or borne from elsewhere one by one. I asked Cruso how many stones had gone into the walls. A hundred thousand or more, he replied. A mighty labour, I remarked. But privately I thought: Is bare earth, baked by the sun and walled about, to be preferred to pebbles and bushes and swarms of birds? "Is it your plan to clear the whole island of growth, and turn it into terraces?" I asked. "It would be the work of many men and many lifetimes to clear the whole island," he replied; by which I saw he chose to understand only the letter of my question. "And what will you be planting, when you plant?" I asked. "The planting is not for us," said he. "We have nothing to plant – that is our misfortune." And he looked at me with such sorry dignity, I could have bit my tongue. "The planting is reserved for those who come after us and have the foresight to bring seed. I only clear the ground for them. Clearing ground and piling stones is little enough, but it is better than sitting in idleness." And then, with great earnestness, he went on: "I ask you to remember, not every man who bears the mark of the castaway is a castaway at heart."

'I reflected long on these words, but they remained dark to me. When I passed the terraces and saw this man, no longer young, labouring in the heat of the day to lift a great stone out of the earth or patiently chopping at the grass, while he waited year after year for some saviour castaway to arrive in a boat with a sack of corn at his feet, I found it a foolish kind of agriculture. It seemed to me he might occupy his time as well in digging for gold, or digging graves first for himself and Friday and then if he wished for all the castaways of the future history of the island, and for me too.

'Time passed with increasing tediousness. When I had exhausted my questions to Cruso about the terraces, and the boat he would not build, and the journal he would not keep, and the tools he would not save from the wreck, and Friday's tongue, there was nothing left to talk of save the weather. Cruso had no stories to tell of the life he had lived as a trader and planter before the shipwreck. He did not care how I came to be in Bahia or what I did there. When I spoke of England and of all the things I intended to see and do when I was rescued, he seemed not to hear me. It was as though he wished his story to begin with his arrival on the island, and mine to begin with my arrival, and the story of us together to end on the island too. Let it not by any means come to pass that Cruso is saved, I reflected to myself; for the world expects stories from its adventurers, better stories than tallies of how many stones they moved in fifteen years, and from where, and to where; Cruso rescued will be a deep disappointment to the world;

the idea of a Cruso on his island is a better thing than the true Cruso tight-lipped and sullen in an alien England.

'I spent my days walking on the cliffs or along the shore, or else sleeping. I did not offer to join Cruso in his work on the terraces, for I held it a stupid labour. I made a cap with flaps to tie over my ears; I wore this, and sometimes closed my ears with plugs too, to shut out the sound of the wind. So I became deaf, as Friday was mute; what difference did it make on an island where no one spoke? The petticoat I had swum ashore in was in tatters. My skin was as brown as an Indian's. I was in the flower of my life, and now this had befallen me. I did not weep; but sometimes I would find myself sitting on the bare earth with my hands over my eyes, rocking back and forth and moaning to myself, and would not know how I had got there. When Friday set food before me I took it with dirty fingers and bolted it like a dog. I squatted in the garden, heedless of who saw me. And I watched and watched the horizon. It mattered not who came, Spaniard or Muscovite or cannibal, so long as I escaped.

'This was the darkest time for me, this time of despair and lethargy; I was as much a burden on Cruso now as he had been on me when he raved with fever.

'Then step by step I recovered my spirits and began to apply myself again to little tasks. Though my heart was no warmer towards Cruso, I was grateful he had suffered my moods and not turned me out.

'Cruso did not use me again. On the contrary, he held himself as distant as if nothing had passed between us. For this I was not sorry. Yet I will confess, had I been convinced I was to spend the rest of my days on the island, I would have offered myself to him again, or importuned him, or done whatever was necessary to conceive and bear a child; for the morose silence which he impressed upon our lives would have driven me mad, to say nothing of the prospect of passing my last years alone with Friday.

'One day I asked Cruso whether there were laws on his island, and what such laws might be; or whether he preferred to follow his inner dictates, trusting his heart to guide him on the path of righteousness.

'"Laws are made for one purpose only," he told me: "to hold us in check when our desires grow immoderate. As long as our desires are moderate we have no need of laws."

'"I have a desire to be saved which I must call immoderate," I said. "It burns in me night and day, I can think of nothing else."

'"I do not wish to hear of your desire," said Cruso. "It concerns other things, it does not concern the island, it is not a matter of the island. On the island there is no law except the law that we shall work for our bread, which is a commandment." And with that he strode away.

'This answer did not satisfy me. If I was but a third mouth to feed, doing no useful labour on the terraces, what held Cruso back from binding me hand and foot and tossing me from the cliffs into the sea? What had held Friday back all these years from beating in his master's head with a stone while he slept, so bringing slavehood to an end and inaugurating a reign of idleness? And what held Cruso back from tying Friday to a post every night, like a dog, to sleep the more secure, or from blinding him, as they blind asses in Brazil? It seemed to me that all things were possible on the island, all tyrannies and cruelties, though in small; and if, in despite of what was possible, we lived at peace one with another, surely this was proof that certain laws unknown to us held sway, or else that we had been following the promptings of our hearts all this time, and our hearts had not betrayed us.

'"How do you punish Friday, when you punish him?" I asked on another occasion.

'"There is no call to punish Friday," replied Cruso. "Friday has lived with me for many years. He has known no other master. He follows me in all things."

'"Yet Friday has lost his tongue," said I, the words uttering themselves.

'"Friday lost his tongue before he became mine," said Cruso, and stared at me in challenge. I was silent. But I thought: We are all punished, every day. This island is our punishment, this island and one another's company, to the death.

'My judgment on Cruso was not always so harsh. One evening, seeing him as he stood on the Bluff with the sun behind him all red and purple, staring out to sea, his staff in his hand and his great conical hat on his head, I thought: He is a truly kingly figure; he is the true king of his island. I thought back to the vale of melancholy through which I had passed, when I had dragged about listlessly, weeping over my misfortune. If I had then known misery, how much deeper must the misery of Cruso not have been in his early days? Might he not justly be deemed a hero who had braved the wilderness and slain the monster of solitude and returned fortified by his victory?

'I used once to think, when I saw Cruso in this evening posture, that, like me, he was searching the horizon for a sail. But I was mistaken. His visits to the Bluff belonged to a practice of losing himself in the contemplation of the wastes of water and sky. Friday never interrupted him during these retreats; when once I innocently approached him, I was rebuffed with angry words, and for days afterwards he and I did not speak. To me, sea and sky remained sea and sky, vacant and tedious. I had not the temperament to love such emptiness.

'I must tell you of the death of Cruso, and of our rescue.

'One morning, a year and more after I became an islander, Friday brought his master home from the terraces weak and fainting. I saw at once the fever had returned. With some foreboding I undressed him and put him to bed and prepared to devote myself to his care, wishing I knew more of cupping and bloodletting.

'This time there was no raving or shouting or struggling. Cruso lay pale as a ghost, a cold sweat standing out on his body, his eyes wide open, his lips sometimes moving, though I could make out no word. I thought: He is a dying man, I cannot save him.

'The very next day, as if the spell of Cruso's gaze on the waters had been broken, a merchantman named the *John* ^H *obart*, making for Bristol with a cargo of cotton and indigo, cast anchor off the island and sent a party ashore. Of this I knew nothing till Friday suddenly came scampering into the hut and snatched up his fishing-spears and dashed off towards the crags where the apes were. Then I came out and saw the ship below, and the sailors in the rigging, and the oars of the rowboat dipping in the waves, and I gave a great cry of joy and fell to my knees.

'Of the arrival of strangers in his kingdom Cruso had his first intimation when three seamen lifted him from his bed into a litter and proceeded to bear him down the path to the shore; and even then he likely thought it all a dream. But when he was hoisted aboard the ^H *obart*, and smelled the tar, and heard the creak of timbers, he came to himself and fought so hard to be free that it took strong men to master him and convey him below.

'"There is another person on the island," I told the ship's-master. "He is a Negro slave, his name is Friday, and he is fled among the crags above the north shore. Nothing you can say will persuade him to yield himself up, for he has no understanding of words or power of speech. It will cost great effort to take him. Nevertheless, I beseech you to send your men ashore again; inasmuch as Friday is a slave and a child, it is our duty to care for him in all things, and not abandon him to a solitude worse than death."

'My plea for Friday was heeded. A new party was sent ashore under the command of the third mate, with orders by no means to harm Friday, since he was a poor simpleton, but to effect what was needed to bring him aboard. I offered to accompany the party, but Captain Smith would not allow this.

'So I sat with the captain in his cabin and ate a plate of salt pork and biscuit, very good after a year of fish, and drank a glass of Madeira, and told him my story, as I have told it to you, which he heard with great attention. "It is a story you should set down in writing and offer to the booksellers," he urged – "There has never before, to my knowledge, been a female castaway of our nation. It will cause a great stir." I shook my head sadly. "As I relate it to you, my story passes the time well enough," I replied; "but what little I know of book-writing tells me its charm will quite vanish when it is set down baldly in print. A liveliness is lost in the writing down which must be supplied by art, and I have no art." "As to art I cannot pronounce, being only a sailor," said Captain Smith; "but you may depend on it, the booksellers will hire a man to set your story to rights, and put in a dash of colour too, here and there." "I will not have any lies told," said I. The captain smiled. "There I cannot vouch for them," he said: "their trade is in books, not in truth." "I would rather be the author of my own story than have lies told about me," I persisted – "If I cannot come forward, as author, and swear to the truth of my tale, what will be the worth of it? I might as well have dreamed it in a snug bed in Chichester."

'At this juncture we were summoned above deck. The landing party was on its way back, and to my joy I made out the dark figure of Friday among the sailors. "Friday, Friday!" I called as the boat came alongside, and smiled to show that all was well, the seamen were friends, not foes. But when he was brought aboard Friday would not meet my eye. With sunken shoulders and bowed head he awaited whatever was to befall him. "Can he not be taken to his master?" I asked the captain — "When he sees Mr Cruso is well cared for, perhaps he will accept that we mean no harm."

'So while sail was hoisted and the head of the ship put about, I led Friday below to the cabin where Cruso lay. "Here is your master, Friday," I said. "He is sleeping, he has taken a sleeping draught. You can see that these are good people. They will bring us back to England, which is your master's home, and there you will be set free. You will discover that life in England is better than life ever was on the island."

'I knew of course that Friday did not understand the words. But it had been my belief from early on that Friday understood tones, that he could hear kindness in a human voice when kindness was sincerely meant. So I went on speaking to him, saying the same words over and over, laying my hand on his arm to soothe him; I guided him to his master's bedside and made him kneel there till I felt calm overtake us, and the sailor who escorted us began to yawn and shuffle.

'It was agreed that I should sleep in Cruso's cabin. As for Friday, I pleaded that he not be quartered with the common seamen. "He would rather sleep on the floor at his master's feet than on the softest bed in Christendom," I said. So Friday was allowed to sleep under the transoms a few paces from the door of Cruso's cabin; from this little den he barely stirred for the duration of the voyage, except when I brought him to visit his master. Whenever I spoke to him I was sure to smile and touch his arm, treating him as we treat a frightened horse. For I saw that the ship and the sailors must be awakening the darkest of memories in him of the time when he was torn from his homeland and transported into captivity in the New World.

'We were used with great civility throughout the voyage. The ship's surgeon visited Cruso twice a day, and by letting blood afforded him much relief. But to me he would privately shake his head. "Your husband is sinking," he would say – "I fear we came too late."

'(I should tell you that Captain Smith had proposed that I call Cruso my husband and declare we had been shipwrecked together, to make my path easier both on board and when we should come ashore in England. If the story of Bahia and the mutineers got about, he said, it would not easily be understood what kind of woman I was. I laughed when he said this – what kind of woman was I, in truth? – but took his advice, and so was known as Mrs Cruso to all on board.

'One night at dinner – I ate all this time at the captain's table – he whispered in my ear that he would be honoured if I would consent to pay him a visit in his cabin afterwards, for a glass of cordial. I pretended to take his offer as mere gallantry, and did not go. He pressed me no further, but continued to behave as courteously as before. In all I found him a true gentleman, though a mere ship's-master and the son of a pedlar, as he told me.)

'I brought Cruso his food in bed and coaxed him to eat as if he were a child. Sometimes he seemed to know where he was, at other times not. One night, hearing him rise, I lit a candle, and saw him standing at the cabin door, pressing against it, not understanding that it opened inwards. I came over to him and touched him, and found his face wet with tears. "Come, my Cruso," I whispered, and guided him back to his bunk, and soothed him till he slept again.

'On the island I believe Cruso might yet have shaken off the fever, as he had done so often before. For though not a young man, he was vigorous. But now he was dying of woe, the extremest woe. With every passing day he was conveyed farther from the kingdom he pined for, to which he would never find his way again. He was a prisoner, and I, despite myself, his gaoler.

'Sometimes in his sleep he would mutter in Portuguese, as he seemed always to do when the bygone past came back to him. Then I would take his hand, or lie beside him and talk to him. "Do you remember, my Cruso," I would say, "how after the great storm had taken away our roof we would lie at night and watch the shooting stars, and wake in the glare of the moon, thinking it was day? In England we will have a roof over our heads that no wind can tear off. But did it not seem to you that the moon of our island was larger than the moon of England, as you remember it, and the stars more numerous? Perhaps we were nearer the moon there, as we were certainly nearer the sun.

'"Yet," I would pursue, "if we were nearer the heavens there, why was it that so little of the island could be called extraordinary? Why were there no strange fruits, no serpents, no lions? Why did the cannibals never come? What will we tell folk in England when they ask us to divert them?"

'"Cruso," I say (it is not the same night, it is a different night, we are ploughing through the waves, the rock of England looms closer and closer), "is there not someone you have forgotten in Brazil? Is there not a sister awaiting your return on your Brazilian estates, and a faithful steward keeping the accounts? Can we not go back to your sister in Brazil, and sleep in hammocks side by side under the great Brazilian sky full of stars?" I lie against Cruso; with the tip of my tongue I follow the hairy whorl of his ear. I rub my cheeks against his harsh whiskers, I spread myself over him, I stroke his body with my thighs. "I am swimming in you, my Cruso," I whisper, and swim. He is a tall man, I a tall woman. This is our coupling: this swimming, this clambering, this whispering.

'Or I speak of the island. "We will visit a corn-factor, I promise, my Cruso," I say. "We will buy a sack of corn, the best there is. We will take ship again for the Americas, and be driven from our course by a storm, and be cast up on your island. We will plant the terraces and make them bloom. We will do all this."

'It is not the words, it is the fervour with which I speak them: Cruso takes my hand between his huge bony hands and brings it to his lips, and weeps.

'We were yet three days from port when Cruso died. I was sleeping beside him in the narrow bunk, and in the night heard him give a long sigh; then afterwards I felt his legs begin to grow cold, and lit the candle and began to chafe his temples and wrists; but by then he was gone. So I went out and spoke to Friday. "Your master is dead, Friday," I whispered.

'Friday lay in his little recess wrapped in the old watch-coat the surgeon had found for him. His eyes glinted in the candlelight but he did not stir. Did he know the meaning of death? No man had died on his island since the beginning of time. Did he know we were subject to death, like the beasts? I held out a hand but he would not take it. So I knew he knew something; though what he knew I did not know.

'Cruso was buried the next day. The crew stood bare-headed, the captain said a prayer, two sailors tilted the bier, and Cruso's remains, sewn in a canvas shroud, with the last stitch through his nose (I saw this done, as did Friday), wrapped about with a great chain, slid into the waves. Throughout the ceremony I felt the curious eyes of the sailors on me (I had seldom been on deck). No doubt I made a strange sight in a dark coat, borrowed from the captain, over sailor's pantaloons and apeskin sandals. Did they truly think of me as Cruso's wife, or had tales already reached them – sailors' haunts are full of gossip – of the Englishwoman from Bahia marooned in the Atlantic by Portuguese mutineers? Do you think of me, Mr Foe, as Mrs Cruso or as a bold adventuress? Think what you may, it was I who shared Cruso's bed and closed Cruso's eyes, as it is I who have disposal of all that Cruso leaves behind, which is the story of his island.'

II

'We are now settled in lodgings in Clock Lane off Long Acre. I go by the name Mrs Cruso, which you should bear in mind. I have a room on the second floor. Friday has a bed in the cellar, where I bring him his meals. By no means could I have abandoned him on the island. Nevertheless, a great city is no place for him. His confusion and distress when I conducted him through the streets this last Saturday wrenched my heartstrings.

'Our lodging is together five shillings a week. Whatever you send I shall be grateful for.

'I have set down the history of our time on the island as well as I can, and enclose it herewith. It is a sorry, limping affair (the history, not the time itself) –"the next day," its refrain goes, "the next day . . . the next day" – but you will know how to set it right.

'You will wonder how I came to choose you, given that a week ago I did not so much as know your name. I admit, when I first laid eyes on you I thought you were a lawyer or a man from the Exchange. But then one of my fellow-servants told me you were Mr Foe the author who had heard many confessions and were reputed a very secret man. It was raining (do you remember?); you paused on the step to fasten your cloak, and I came out too and shut the door behind me. "If I may be so bold, sir," I said (those were the words, bold words). You looked me up and down but did not reply, and I thought to myself: What art is there to hearing confessions? – the spider has as much art, that watches and waits. "If I may have a moment of your time: I am seeking a new situation." "So are we all seeking a new situation," you replied. "But I have a man to care for, a Negro man who can never find a situation, since he has lost his tongue," I said – "I hoped that you might have place for me, and for him too, in your establishment." My hair was wet by now, I had not even a shawl. Rain dripped from the brim of your hat. "I am in employ here, but am used to better things," I pursued – "You have not heard a story before like mine. I am new-returned from far-off parts. I have been a castaway on a desert island. And there I was the companion of a singular man." I smiled, not at you but at what I was about to say. "I am a figure of fortune, Mr Foe. I am the good fortune we are always hoping for."

'Was it effrontery to say that? Was it effrontery to smile? Was it the effrontery that aroused your interest?'

'Thank you for the three guineas. I have bought Friday a drayer's woollen jerkin, also woollen hose. If there is underlinen you can spare, I should welcome it. He wears clothes without murmur, though he will not yet wear shoes.

'Can you not take us into your house? Why do you keep me apart? Can you not take me in as your close servant, and Friday as your gardener?

'I climb the staircase (it is a tall house, tall and airy, with many flights of stairs) and tap at the door. You are sitting at a table with your back to me, a rug over your knees, your feet in pantoufles, gazing out over the fields, thinking, stroking your chin with your pen, waiting for me to set down the tray and withdraw. On the tray are a glassful of hot water into which I have squeezed a citron, and two slices of buttered toast. You call it your first breakfast.

'The room is barely furnished. The truth is, it is not a room but a part of the attic to which you remove yourself for the sake of silence. The table and chair stand on a platform of boards before the window. From the door of the attic to this platform, boards are laid to form a narrow walk-way. Otherwise there are only the ceiling-boards, on which one treads at one's peril, and the rafters, and overhead the grey rooftiles. Dust lies thick on the floor; when the wind gusts under the eaves there are flurries in the dust, and from the corners moaning noises. There are mice too. Before you go downstairs you must shut your papers away to preserve them from the mice. In the mornings you brush mouse-droppings from the table.

'There is a ripple in the window-pane. Moving your head, you can make the ripple travel over the cows grazing in the pasture, over the ploughed land beyond, over the line of poplars, and up into the sky.

'I think of you as a steersman steering the great hulk of the house through the nights and days, peering ahead for signs of storm.

'Your papers are kept in a chest beside the table. The story of Cruso's island will go there page by page as you write it, to lie with a heap of other papers: a census of the beggars of London, bills of mortality from the time of the great plague, accounts of travels in the border country, reports of strange and surprising apparitions, records of the wool trade, a memorial of the life and opinions of Dickory Cronke (who is he?); also books of voyages to the New World, memoirs of captivity among the Moors, chronicles of the wars in the Low Countries, confessions of notorious lawbreakers, and a multitude of castaway narratives, most of them, I would guess, riddled with lies.

'When I was on the island I longed only to be elsewhere, or, in the word I then used, to be saved. But now a longing stirs in me I never thought I would feel. I close my eyes and my soul takes leave of me, flying over the houses and streets, the woods and pastures, back to our old home, Cruso's and mine. You will not understand this longing, after all I have said of the tedium of our life there. Perhaps I should have written more about the pleasure I took in walking barefoot in the cool sand of the compound, more about the birds, the little birds of many varieties whose names I never knew, whom I called sparrows for want of a better name. Who but Cruso, who is no more, could truly tell you Cruso's story? I should have said less about him, more about myself. How, to begin with, did my daughter come to be lost, and how, following her, did I reach Bahia? How did I survive among strangers those two long years? Did I live only in a rooming-house, as I have said? Was Bahia an island in the ocean of the Brazilian forest, and my room a lonely island in Bahia? Who was the captain whose fate it became to drift forever in the south-ernmost seas, clothed in ice? I brought back not a feather, not a thimbleful of sand, from Cruso's island. All I have is my sandals. When I reflect on my story I seem to exist only as the one who came, the one who witnessed, the one who longed to be gone: a being without substance, a ghost beside the true body of Cruso. Is that the fate of all storytellers? Yet I was as much a body as Cruso. I ate and drank, I woke and slept, I longed. The island was Cruso's (yet by what right? by the law of islands? is there such a law?), but I lived there too, I was no bird of passage, no gannet or albatross, to circle the island once and dip a wing and then fly on over the boundless ocean. Return to me the substance I have lost, Mr Foe: that is my entreaty. For though my story gives the truth, it does not give the substance of the truth (I see that clearly, we need not pretend it is otherwise). To tell the truth in all its substance you must have quiet, and a com-fortable chair away from all distraction, and a window

to stare through; and then the knack of seeing waves
when there are fields before your eyes, and of feeling
the tropic sun when it is cold; and at your fingertips
the words with which to capture the vision before it
fades. I have none of these, while you have all.'

'*April 21st*

'In my letter yesterday I may have seemed to mock
the art of writing. I ask your pardon, I was unjust.
Believe me, there are times when, as I think of you
labouring in your attic to bring life to your thieves
and courtesans and grenadiers, my heart aches with
pity and I long only to be of service. I think of you
(forgive me the figure) as a beast of burden, and your
house as a great wagon you are condemned to haul, a
wagon full of tables and chairs and wardrobes, and on
top of these a wife (I do not even know whether you
have a wife!) and ungrateful children and idle servants
and cats and dogs, all eating your victuals, burning
your coal, yawning and laughing, careless of your toil.
In the early mornings, lying in my warm bed, I seem
to hear the shuffle of your footsteps as, draped in a
rug, you climb the stairs to your attic. You seat yourself, your breathing is heavy, you light the lamp, you
pinch your eyes shut and begin to grope your way
back to where you were last night, through the dark
and cold, through the rain, over fields where sheep lie
huddled together, over forests, over the seas, to
Flanders or wherever it is that your captains and

grenadiers must now too begin to stir and set about the next day in their lives, while from the corners of the attic the mice stare at you, twitching their whiskers. Even on Sundays the work proceeds, as though whole regiments of foot would sink into everlasting sleep were they not roused daily and sent into action. In the throes of a chill you plod on, wrapped in scarves, blowing your nose, hawking, spitting. Sometimes you are so weary that the candlelight swims before your eyes. You lay your head on your arms and in a moment are asleep, a black stripe across the paper where the pen slips from your grasp. Your mouth sags open, you snore softly, you smell (forgive me a second time) like an old man. How I wish it were in my power to help you, Mr Foe! Closing my eyes, I gather my strength and send out a vision of the island to hang before you like a substantial body, with birds and fleas and fish of all hues and lizards basking in the sun, flicking out their black tongues, and rocks covered in barnacles, and rain drumming on the roof-fronds, and wind, unceasing wind: so that it will be there for you to draw on whenever you have need.'

'*April 25th*

'You asked how it was that Cruso did not save a single musket from the wreck; why a man so fearful of cannibals should have neglected to arm himself.

'Cruso never showed me where the wreck lay, but it is my conviction that it lay, and lies still, in the deep water below the cliffs in the north of the island. At the height of the storm Cruso leapt overboard with the youthful Friday at his side, and other shipmates too, it may be; but they two alone were saved, by a great wave that caught them up and bore them ashore. Now I ask: Who can keep powder dry in the belly of a wave? Furthermore: Why should a man endeavour to save a musket when he barely hopes to save his own life? As for cannibals, I am not persuaded, despite Cruso's fears, that there are cannibals in those oceans. You may with right reply that, as we do not expect to see sharks dancing in the waves, so we should not expect to see cannibals dancing on the strand; that cannibals belong to the night as sharks belong to the depths. All I say is: What I saw, I wrote. I saw no cannibals; and if they came after nightfall and fled before the dawn, they left no footprint behind.

'I dreamed last night of Cruso's death, and woke with tears coursing down my cheeks. So I lay a long while, the grief not lifting from my heart. Then I went downstairs to our little courtyard off Clock Lane. It was not yet light; the sky was clear. Under these same tranquil stars, I thought, floats the island where we lived; and on that island is a hut, and in that hut a bed of soft grass which perhaps still bears the imprint, fainter every day, of my body. Day by day the wind picks at the roof and the weeds creep across the terraces. In a year, in ten years, there will be nothing left standing but a circle of sticks to mark the place where the hut stood, and of the terraces only the walls. And of the walls they will say, These are cannibal walls, the ruins of a cannibal city, from the golden age of the cannibals. For who will believe they were built by one man and a slave, in the hope that one day a seafarer would come with a sack of corn for them to sow?

'You remarked it would have been better had Cruso rescued not only musket and powder and ball, but a carpenter's chest as well, and built himself a boat. I do not wish to be captious, but we lived on an island so buffeted by the wind that there was not a tree did not grow twisted and bent. We might have built a raft, a crooked kind of raft, but never a boat.

'You asked also after Cruso's apeskin clothes. Alas, these were taken from our cabin and tossed overboard by ignorant sailors. If you so desire, I will make sketches of us as we were on the island, wearing the clothes we wore.

'The sailor's blouse and pantaloons I wore on board ship I have given to Friday. Moreover he has his jerkin and his watch-coat. His cellar gives on to the yard, so he is free to wander as he pleases. But he rarely goes abroad, being too fearful. How he fills his time I do not know, for the cellar is bare save for his cot and the coal-bin and some broken sticks of furniture.

'Yet the story that there is a cannibal in Clock Lane has plainly got about, for yesterday I found three boys at the cellar door peering in on Friday. I chased them off, after which they took up their stand at the end of the lane, chanting the words: "Cannibal Friday, have you ate your mam today?"

'Friday grows old before his time, like a dog locked up all its life. I too, from living with an old man and sleeping in his bed, have grown old. There are times when I think of myself as a widow. If there was a wife left behind in Brazil, she and I would be sisters now, of a kind.

'I have the use of the scullery two mornings of the week, and am turning Friday into a laundryman; for otherwise idleness will destroy him. I set him before the sink dressed in his sailor clothes, his feet bare as ever on the cold floor (he will not wear shoes). "Watch me, Friday!" I say, and begin to soap a petticoat (soap must be introduced to him, there was no soap in his life before, on the island we used ash or sand), and rub it on the washing-board. "Now *do*, Friday!" I say, and stand aside. *Watch* and *Do*: those are my two principal words for Friday, and with them I accomplish much. It is a terrible fall, I know, from the freedom of the island where he could roam all day, and hunt birds' eggs, and spear fish, when the terraces did not call. But surely it is better to learn useful tasks than to lie alone in a cellar all day, thinking I know not what thoughts?

'Cruso would not teach him because, he said, Friday had no need of words. But Cruso erred. Life on the island, before my coming, would have been less tedious had he taught Friday to understand his meanings, and devised ways by which Friday could express his own meanings, as for example by gesturing with his hands or by setting out pebbles in shapes standing for words. Then Cruso might have spoken to Friday after his manner, and Friday responded after his, and many an empty hour been whiled away. For I cannot believe that the life Friday led before he fell into Cruso's hands was bereft of interest, though he was but a child. I would give much to hear the truth of how he was captured by the slave-traders and lost his tongue.

'He is become a great lover of oatmeal, gobbling down as much porridge in a day as would feed a dozen Scotsmen. From eating too much and lying abed he is growing stupid. Seeing him with his belly tight as a drum and his thin shanks and his listless air, you would not believe he was the same man who brief months ago stood poised on the rocks, the seaspray dancing about him, the sunlight glancing on his limbs, his spear raised, ready in an instant to strike a fish.

'While he works I teach him the names of things. I hold up a spoon and say "Spoon, Friday!" and give the spoon into his hand. Then I say "Spoon!" and hold out my hand to receive the spoon; hoping thus that in time the word *Spoon* will echo in his mind willy-nilly whenever his eye falls on a spoon.

'What I fear most is that after years of speechlessness the very notion of speech may be lost to him. When I take the spoon from his hand (but is it truly a spoon to him, or a mere thing? – I do not know), and say *Spoon*, how can I be sure he does not think I am chattering to myself as a magpie or an ape does, for the pleasure of hearing the noise I make, and feeling the play of my tongue, as he himself used to find pleasure in playing his flute? And whereas one may take a dull child and twist his arm or pinch his ear till at last he repeats after us, *Spoon*, what can I do with Friday? "Spoon, Friday!" I say; "Fork! Knife!" I think of the root of his tongue closed behind those heavy lips like a toad in eternal winter, and I shiver. "Broom,

Friday!" I say, and make motions of sweeping, and press the broom into his hand.

'Or I bring a book to the scullery. "This is a book, Friday," I say. "In it is a story written by the renowned Mr Foe. You do not know the gentleman, but at this very moment he is engaged in writing another story, which is your story, and your master's, and mine. Mr Foe has not met you, but he knows of you, from what I have told him, using words. That is part of the magic of words. Through the medium of words I have given Mr Foe the particulars of you and Mr Cruso and of my year on the island and the years you and Mr Cruso spent there alone, as far as I can supply them; and all these particulars Mr Foe is weaving into a story which will make us famous throughout the land, and rich too. There will be no more need for you to live in a cellar. You will have money with which to buy your way to Africa or Brazil, as the desire moves you, bearing fine gifts, and be reunited with your parents, if they remember you, and marry at last and have children, sons and daughters. And I will give you your own copy of our book, bound in leather, to take with you. I will show you how to trace your name in it, page after page, so that your children may see that their father is known in all parts of the world where books are read. Is writing not a fine thing, Friday? Are you not filled with joy to know that you will live forever, after a manner?"

'Having introduced you thus, I open your book and read from it to Friday. "This is the story of Mrs Veal, another humble person whom Mr Foe has made famous in the course of his writing," I say. "Alas, we shall never meet Mrs Veal, for she has passed away; and as to her friend Mrs Barfield, she lives in Canterbury, a city some distance to the south of us on this island where we find ourselves, named Britain; I doubt we shall ever go there."

'Through all my chatter Friday labours away at the washing-board. I expect no sign that he has understood. It is enough to hope that if I make the air around him thick with words, memories will be reborn in him which died under Cruso's rule, and with them the recognition that to live in silence is to live like the whales, great castles of flesh floating leagues apart one from another, or like the spiders, sitting each alone at the heart of his web, which to him is the entire world. Friday may have lost his tongue but he has not lost his ears – that is what I say to myself. Through his ears Friday may yet take in the wealth stored in stories and so learn that the world is not, as the island seemed to teach him, a barren and a silent place (is that the secret meaning of the word story, do you think: a storing-place of memories?).

'I watch his toes curl on the floorboards or the cobblestones and know that he craves the softness of earth under his feet. How I wish there were a garden I could take him to! Could he and I not visit your garden in Stoke Newington? We should be as quiet as ghosts. "Spade, Friday!" I should whisper, offering the spade to his hand; and then: "Dig!" – which is a word his master taught him – "Turn over the soil, pile up the weeds for burning. Feel the spade. Is it not a fine, sharp tool? It is an English spade, made in an English smithy."

'So, watching his hand grip the spade, watching his eyes, I seek the first sign that he comprehends what I am attempting: not to have the beds cleared (I am sure you have your own gardener), not even to save him from idleness, or for the sake of his health to bring him out of the dankness of his cellar, but to build a bridge of words over which, when one day it is grown sturdy enough, he may cross to the time before Cruso, the time before he lost his tongue, when he lived immersed in the prattle of words as unthinking as a fish in water; from where he may by steps return, as far as he is able, to the world of words in which you, Mr Foe, and I, and other people live.

'Or I bring out your shears and show him their use. "Here in England," I say, "it is our custom to grow hedges to mark the limits of our property. Doubtless that would not be possible in the forests of Africa. But here we grow hedges, and then cut them straight, so that our gardens shall be neatly marked out." I lop at the hedge till it becomes clear to Friday what I am doing: not cutting a passage through your hedge, not cutting down your hedge, but cutting one side of it straight. "Now, Friday, take the shears," I say: "Cut!"; and Friday takes the shears and cuts in a clean line, as I know he is capable of doing, for his digging is impeccable.

'I tell myself I talk to Friday to educate him out of darkness and silence. But is that the truth? There are times when benevolence deserts me and I use words only as the shortest way to subject him to my will. At such times I understand why Cruso preferred not to disturb his muteness. I understand, that is to say, why

a man will choose to be a slaveowner. Do you think
less of me for this confession?'

'*April 28th*

'My letter of the 25th is returned unopened. I pray
there has been some simple mistake. I enclose the
same herewith.'

'*May 1st*

'I have visited Stoke Newington and found the bailiffs
in occupation of your house. It is a cruel thing to say,
but I almost laughed to learn this was the reason for
your silence, you had not lost interest and turned your
back on us. Yet now I must ask myself: Where shall I
send my letters? Will you continue to write our story
while you are in hiding? Will you still contribute to
our keep? Are Friday and I the only personages you
have settled in lodgings while you write their story,
or are there many more of us dispersed about London
– old campaigners from the wars in Italy, cast-off
mistresses, penitent highwaymen, prosperous thieves?
How will you live while you are in hiding? Have you
a woman to cook your meals and wash your linen?
Can your neighbours be trusted? Remember: the bailiffs have their spies everywhere. Be wary of public
houses. If you are harried, come to Clock Lane.'

'I must disclose I have twice been to your house in the past week in the hope of hearing tidings. Do not be annoyed. I have not revealed to Mrs Thrush who I am. I say only that I have messages for you, messages of the utmost importance. On my first visit Mrs Thrush plainly gave to know she did not believe me. But my earnestness has now won her over. She has accepted my letters, promising to keep them safe, which I take to be a manner of saying she will send them to you. Am I right? Do they reach you? She confides that she frets for your welfare and longs for the departure of the bailiffs.

'The bailiffs have quartered themselves in your library. One sleeps on the couch, the other, it seems, in two armchairs drawn together. They send out to the King's Arms for their meals. They are prepared to wait a month, two months, a year, they say, to serve their warrant. A month I can believe, but not a year – they do not know how long a year can be. It was one of them, an odious fellow named Wilkes, who opened the door to me the second time. He fancies I carry messages between you and Mrs Thrush. He pinned me in the passageway before I left and told me of the Fleet, of how men have spent their lives there abandoned by their families, castaways in the very heart of the city. Who will save you, Mr Foe, if you are arrested and consigned to the Fleet? I thought you had a wife, but Mrs Thrush says you are widowed many years.

'Your library reeks of pipesmoke. The door of the

larger cabinet is broken and the glass not so much as swept up. Mrs Thrush says that Wilkes and his friend had a woman with them last night.

'I came home to Clock Lane in low spirits. There are times when I feel my strength to be limitless, when I can bear you and your troubles on my back, and the bailiffs as well if need be, and Friday and Cruso and the island. But there are other times when a pall of weariness falls over me and I long to be borne away to a new life in a far-off city where I will never hear your name or Cruso's again. Can you not press on with your writing, Mr Foe, so that Friday can speedily be returned to Africa and I liberated from this drab existence I lead? Hiding from the bailiffs is surely tedious, and writing a better way than most of passing the time. The memoir I wrote for you I wrote sitting on my bed with the paper on a tray on my knees, my heart fearful all the while that Friday would decamp from the cellar to which he had been consigned, or take a stroll and be lost in the mazes and warrens of Covent Garden. Yet I completed that memoir in three days. More is at stake in the history you write, I will admit, for it must not only tell the truth about us but please its readers too. Will you not bear it in mind, however, that my life is drearily suspended till your writing is done?'

'May 19th

'The days pass and I have no word from you. A patch of dandelions – all we have for flowers in Clock Lane – is pushing up against the wall beneath my window. By noon the room is hot. I will stifle if summer comes and I am still confined. I long for the ease of walking abroad in my shift, as I did on the island.

'The three guineas you sent are spent. Clothes for Friday were a heavy expense. The rent for this week is owed. I am ashamed to come downstairs and cook our poor supper of peas and salt.

'To whom am I writing? I blot the pages and toss them out of the window. Let who will read them.'

*   *

'The house in Newington is closed up, Mrs Thrush and the servants are departed. When I pronounce your name the neighbours grow tight-lipped. What has happened? Have the bailiffs tracked you down? Will you be able to proceed with your writing in prison?'

'May 29th

'We have taken up residence in your house, from which I now write. Are you surprised to hear this? There were spider-webs over the windows already, which we have swept away. We will disturb nothing. When you return we will vanish like ghosts, without complaint.

'I have your table to sit at, your window to gaze through. I write with your pen on your paper, and when the sheets are completed they go into your chest. So your life continues to be lived, though you are gone.

'All I lack is light. There is not a candle left in the house. But perhaps that is a blessing. Since we must keep the curtains drawn, we will grow used to living in gloom by day, in darkness by night.

'It is not wholly as I imagined it would be. What I thought would be your writing-table is not a table but a bureau. The window overlooks not woods and pastures but your garden. There is no ripple in the glass. The chest is not a true chest but a dispatch box. Nevertheless, it is all close enough. Does it surprise you as much as it does me, this correspondence between things as they are and the pictures we have of them in our minds?'

*   *

'We have explored your garden, Friday and I. The flower-beds are sadly overgrown, but the carrots and beans are prospering. I will set Friday to work weeding.

'We live here like the humblest of poor relations. Your best linen is put away; we eat off the servants' plate. Think of me as the niece of a second cousin come down in the world, to whom you owe but the barest of duties.

'I pray you have not taken the step of embarking for the colonies. My darkest fear is that an Atlantic storm will drive your ship on to uncharted rocks and spill you up on a barren isle.

'There was a time in Clock Lane, I will confess, when I felt great bitterness against you. He has turned his mind from us, I told myself, as easily as if we were two of his grenadiers in Flanders, forgetting that while his grenadiers fall into an enchanted sleep whenever he absents himself, Friday and I continue to eat and drink and fret. There seemed no course open to me but to take to the streets and beg, or steal, or worse. But now that we are in your house, peace has returned. Why it should be so I do not know, but toward this house – which till last month I had never clapped eyes on – I feel as we feel toward the home we were born in. All the nooks and crannies, all the odd hidden corners of the garden, have an air of familiarity, as if in a forgotten childhood I here played games of hide and seek.'

*   *

'How much of my life consists in waiting! In Bahia I did little but wait, though what I was waiting for I sometimes did not know. On the island I waited all the time for rescue. Here I wait for you to appear, or for the book to be written that will set me free of Cruso and Friday.

'I sat at your bureau this morning (it is afternoon now, I sit at the same bureau, I have sat here all day) and took out a clean sheet of paper and dipped pen in ink – your pen, your ink, I know, but somehow the pen becomes mine while I write with it, as though growing out of my hand – and wrote at the head: "The Female Castaway. Being a True Account of a Year Spent on a Desert Island. With Many Strange Circumstances Never Hitherto Related." Then I made a list of all the strange circumstances of the year I could remember: the mutiny and murder on the Portuguese ship, Cruso's castle, Cruso himself with his lion's mane and apeskin clothes, his voiceless slave Friday, the vast terraces they had built, all bare of growth, the terrible storm that tore the roof off our house and heaped the beaches with dying fish. Dubiously I thought: Are these enough strange circumstances to make a story of? How long before I am driven to invent new and stranger circumstances: the salvage of tools and muskets from Cruso's ship; the building of a boat, or at least a skiff, and a venture to sail to the mainland; a landing by cannibals on the island, followed by a skirmish and many bloody deaths; and, at last, the coming of a golden-haired stranger with a sack of corn, and the planting of the terraces? Alas, will the day ever arrive when we can make a story without strange circumstances?

'Then there is the matter of Friday's tongue. On the island I accepted that I should never learn how Friday lost his tongue, as I accepted that I should never learn how the apes crossed the sea. But what we can accept in life we cannot accept in history. To tell my story and be silent on Friday's tongue is no better than offering a book for sale with pages in it quietly left empty. Yet the only tongue that can tell Friday's secret is the tongue he has lost!

'So this morning I made two sketches. One showed

the figure of a man clad in jerkin and drawers and a conical hat, with whiskers standing out in all directions and great cat-eyes. Kneeling before him was the figure of a black man, naked save for drawers, holding his hands behind his back (the hands were tied, but that could not be seen). In his left hand the whiskered figure gripped the living tongue of the other; in his right hand he held up a knife.

'Of the second sketch I will tell you in a moment.

'I took my sketches down to Friday in the garden. "Consider these pictures, Friday," I said, "then tell me: which is the truth?" I held up the first. "Master Cruso," I said, pointing to the whiskered figure. "Friday," I said, pointing to the kneeling figure. "Knife," I said, pointing to the knife. "Cruso cut out Friday's tongue," I said; and I stuck out my own tongue and made motions of cutting it. "Is that the truth, Friday?" I pressed him, looking deep into his eyes: "Master Cruso cut out your tongue?"

'(Friday might not know the meaning of the word *truth*, I reasoned; nevertheless, if my picture stirred some recollection of the truth, surely a cloud would pass over his gaze; for are the eyes not rightly called the mirrors of the soul?)

'Yet even as I spoke I began to doubt myself. For if Friday's gaze indeed became troubled, might that not be because I came striding out of the house, demanding that he look at pictures, something I had never done before? Might the picture itself not confuse him? (For, examining it anew, I recognized with chagrin that it might also be taken to show Cruso as a beneficent father putting a lump of fish into the mouth of child Friday.) And how did he understand my gesture of putting out my tongue at him? What if, among the cannibals of Africa, putting out the tongue has the same meaning as offering the lips has amongst us? Might you not then flush with shame when a woman puts out her tongue and you have no tongue with which to respond?

'I brought out my second sketch. Again there was depicted little Friday, his arms stretched behind him, his mouth wide open; but now the man with the knife was a slave-trader, a tall black man clad in a burnous, and the knife was sickle-shaped. Behind this Moor waved the palm-trees of Africa. "Slave-trader," I said, pointing to the man. "Man who catches boys and sells them as slaves. Did a slave-trader cut out your tongue, Friday? Was it a slave-trader or Master Cruso?"

'But Friday's gaze remained vacant, and I began to grow disheartened. Who, after all, was to say he did not lose his tongue at the age when boy-children among the Jews are cut; and, if so, how could he remember the loss? Who was to say there do not exist entire tribes in Africa among whom the men are mute and speech is reserved to women? Why should it not be so? The world is more various than we ever give it credit for – that is one of the lessons I was taught by Bahia. Why should such tribes not exist, and procreate, and flourish, and be content?

'Or if there was indeed a slave-trader, a Moorish slave-trader with a hooked knife, was my picture of him at all like the Moor Friday remembered? Are Moors all tall and clad in white burnouses? Perhaps the Moor gave orders to a trusty slave to cut out the tongues of the captives, a wizened black slave in a loin-cloth. "Is this a faithful representation of the man who cut out your tongue?" – was that what Friday, in his way, understood me to be asking? If so, what answer could he give but No? And even if it was a Moor who cut out his tongue, his Moor was likely an inch taller than mine, or an inch shorter; wore black or blue, not white; was bearded, not clean-shaven; had a straight knife, not a curved one; and so forth.

'So, standing before Friday, I slowly tore up my pictures. A long silence fell. For the first time I noted how long Friday's fingers were, folded on the shaft of the spade. "Ah, Friday!" I said. "Shipwreck is a great leveller, and so is destitution, but we are not level enough yet." And then, though no reply came nor ever would, I went on, giving voice to all that lay in my heart. "I am wasting my life on you, Friday, on you and your foolish story. I mean no hurt, but it is true. When I am an old woman I will look back on this as a great waste of time, a time of being wasted by time. What are we doing here, you and I, among the sober burgesses of Newington, waiting for a man who will never come back?"

'If Friday had been anyone else, I would have wished him to take me in his arms and comfort me, for seldom had I felt so miserable. But Friday stood like a statue. I have no doubt that amongst Africans the human sympathies move as readily as amongst us. But the unnatural years Friday had spent with Cruso had deadened his heart, making him cold, incurious, like an animal wrapt entirely in itself.'

'During the reign of the bailiffs, as you will understand, the neighbours shunned your house. But today
a gentleman who introduced himself as Mr Summers
called. I thought it prudent to tell him I was the new
housekeeper and Friday the gardener. I was plausible
enough, I believe, to convince him we are not gipsies
who have chanced on an empty house and settled in.
The house itself is clean and neat, even the library,
and Friday was at work in the garden, so the lie did
not seem too great.

'I wonder sometimes whether you do not wait im-
patiently in your quarter of London for tidings that
the castaways are at last flitten and you are free to
come home. Do you have spies who peer in at the
windows to see whether we are still in occupation?
Do you pass by the house yourself daily in thick
disguise? Is the truth that your hiding-place is not in
the back alleys of Shoreditch or Whitechapel, as we all
surmise, but in this sunny village itself? Is Mr
Summers of your party? Have you taken up residence
in his attic, where you pass the time perusing through
a spyglass the life we lead? If so, you will believe me
when I say the life we lead grows less and less distinct
from the life we led on Cruso's island. Sometimes I
wake up not knowing where I am. The world is full
of islands, said Cruso once. His words ring truer every
day.

'I write my letters, I seal them, I drop them in the
box. One day when we are departed you will tip them
out and glance through them. "Better had there been

only Cruso and Friday," you will murmur to yourself: "Better without the woman." Yet where would you be without the woman? Would Cruso have come to you of his own accord? Could you have made up Cruso and Friday and the island with its fleas and apes and lizards? I think not. Many strengths you have, but invention is not one of them.'

* *

'A stranger has been watching the house, a girl. She stands across the street for hours on end, making no effort to conceal herself. Passers-by stop and talk to her, but she ignores them. I ask: Is she another of the bailiffs' spies, or is she sent by you to observe us? She wears a grey cloak and cape, despite the summer's heat, and carries a basket.

'I went out to her today, the fourth day of her vigil. "Here is a letter for your masters," I said, without preamble, and dropped a letter in her basket. She stared in surprise. Later I found the letter pushed back under the door unopened. I had addressed it to Wilkes the bailiff. If the girl were in the bailiffs' service, I reasoned, she could not refuse to take a letter to them. So I tied in a packet all the letters I had written you and went out a second time.

'It was late in the afternoon. She stood before me stiff as a statue, wrapped in her cloak. "When you see Mr Foe, give him these," I said, and presented the letters. She shook her head. "Will you not see Mr Foe then?" I asked. Again she shook her head. "Who are you? Why do you watch Mr Foe's house?" I pursued, wondering whether I had to do with another mute.

'She raised her head. "Do you not know who I am?" she said. Her voice was low, her lip trembled.

'"I have never set eyes on you in my life," said I.

'All the colour drained from her face. "That is not true," she whispered; and let fall the hood of her cape and shook free her hair, which was hazel-brown.

'"Tell me your name and I will know better," said I.

'"My name is Susan Barton," she whispered; by which I knew I was conversing with a madwoman.

'"And why do you watch my house all day, Susan Barton?" I asked, holding my voice level.

'"To speak with you," she replied.

'"And what is my name?"

'"Your name is Susan Barton too."

'"And who sends you to watch my house? Is it Mr Foe? Does Mr Foe wish us to be gone?"

'"I know no Mr Foe," said she. "I come only to see you."

'"And what may your business be with me?"

'"Do you not know," said she, in a voice so low I could barely hear – "Do you not know whose child I am?"

'"I have never set eyes on you in my life," said I. "Whose child are you?" To which she made no reply, but bowed her head and began to weep, standing clumsily with her hands at her sides, her basket at her feet.

'Thinking, This is some poor lost child who does not know who she is, I put an arm about her to comfort her. But as I touched her she of a sudden dropped to her knees and embraced me, sobbing as if her heart would break.

'"What is it, child?" said I, trying to break her grip on me.

'"You do not know me, you do not know me!" she cried.

'"It is true I do not know you, but I know your name, you told me, it is Susan Barton, the same name as mine."

'At this she wept even harder. "You have forgotten me!" she sobbed.

'"I have not forgotten you, for I never knew you. But you must get up and dry your tears."

'She allowed me to raise her, and took my hand-kerchief and dried her eyes and blew her nose. I thought: What a great blubbering lump! "Now you must tell me," said I: "How do you come to know my name?" (For to Mr Summers I presented myself simply as the new housekeeper; to no one in Newington have I given my name.)

'"I have followed you everywhere," said the girl.

'"Everywhere?" said I, smiling.

'"Everywhere," said she.

'"I know of one place where you have not followed me," said I.

'"I have followed you everywhere," said she.

'"Did you follow me across the ocean?" said I.

'"I know of the island," said she.

'It was as if she had struck me in the face. "You know nothing of the island," I retorted.

'"I know of Bahia too. I know you were scouring Bahia for me."

74

'By these words she betrayed from whom she had her intelligence. Burning with anger against her and against you, I turned on my heel and slammed the door behind me. For an hour she waited at her post, then toward evening departed.

'Who is she and why do you send her to me? Is she sent as a sign you are alive? She is not my daughter. Do you think women drop children and forget them as snakes lay eggs? Only a man could entertain such a fancy. If you want me to quit the house, give the order and I will obey. Why send a child in an old woman's clothes, a child with a round face and a little O of a mouth and a story of a lost mother? She is more your daughter than she ever was mine.'

*   *

'A brewer. She says that her father was a brewer. That she was born in Deptford in May of 1702. That I am her mother. We sit in your drawing-room and I explain to her that I have never lived in Deptford in my life, that I have never known a brewer, that I have a daughter, it is true, but my daughter is lost, she is not that daughter. Sweetly she shakes her head and begins a second time the story of the brewer George Lewes my husband. "Then your name is Lewes, if that is the name of your father," I interrupt. "It may be my name in law but it is not my name in truth," says she. "If we were to be speaking of names in truth," say I, "my name would not be Barton." "That is not what I mean," says she. "Then what do you mean?" say I. "I

am speaking of our true names, our veritable names,"
says she.

'She returns to the story of the brewer. The brewer
haunts gaming-houses and loses his last penny. He
borrows money and loses that too. To escape his
creditors he flees England and enlists as a grenadier in
the Low Countries, where he is later rumoured to
perish. I am left destitute with a daughter to care for.
I have a maidservant named Amy or Emmy. Amy or
Emmy asks my daughter what life she means to follow
when she grows up (this is her earliest memory). She
replies in her childish way that she means to be a
gentlewoman. Amy or Emmy laughs: Mark my words,
Amy says, the day will yet arrive when we three shall
be servants together. "I have never had a servant in
my life, whether named Amy or Emmy or anything
else," I say. (Friday was not my slave but Cruso's, and
is a free man now. He cannot even be said to be a
servant, so idle is his life.) "You confuse me with
some other person."

'She smiles again and shakes her head. "Behold the
sign by which we may know our true mother," she
says, and leans forward and places her hand beside
mine. "See," she says, "we have the same hand. The
same hand and the same eyes."

'I stare at the two hands side by side. My hand is
long, hers short. Her fingers are the plump unformed
fingers of a child. Her eyes are grey, mine brown.
What kind of being is she, so serenely blind to the
evidence of her senses?

'"Did a man send you here?" I ask – "A gentleman
of middle height, with a mole on his chin, here?"

'"No," she says.

'"I do not believe you," I say. "I believe you were sent here, and now I am sending you away. I request you to go away and not to trouble me again."

'She shakes her head and grips the arm of her chair. The air of calm vanishes. "I will not be sent away!" she says through clenched teeth.

'"Very well," say I, "if you wish to stay, stay." And I withdraw, locking the door behind me and pocketing the key.

'In the hallway I encounter Friday standing listlessly in a corner (he stands always in corners, never in the open: he mistrusts space). "It is nothing, Friday," I tell him. "It is only a poor mad girl come to join us. In Mr Foe's house there are many mansions. We are as yet only a castaway and a dumb slave and now a madwoman. There is place yet for lepers and acrobats and pirates and whores to join our menagerie. But pay no heed to me. Go back to bed and sleep." And I brush past him.

'I talk to Friday as old women talk to cats, out of loneliness, till at last they are deemed to be witches, and shunned in the streets.

'Later I return to the drawing-room. The girl is sitting in an armchair, her basket at her feet, knitting. "You will harm your eyesight, knitting in this light," I say. She lays down her knitting. "There is one circumstance you misunderstand," I continue. "The world is full of stories of mothers searching for sons and daughters they gave away once, long ago. But there are no stories of daughters searching for mothers.

There are no stories of such quests because they do not occur. They are not part of life."

'"You are mistaken," says she. "You are my mother, I have found you, and now I will not leave you."

'"I will admit I have indeed lost a daughter. But I did not give her away, she was taken from me, and you are not she. I am leaving the door unlocked. Depart when you are ready."

'This morning when I come downstairs she is still there, sprawled in the armchair, bundled in her cloak, asleep. Bending over her I see that one eye is half open and the eyeball rolled back. I shake her. "It is time to go," I say. "No," says she. Nevertheless, from the kitchen I hear the door close and the latch click behind her.

'"Who brought you up after I abandoned you?" I asked. "The gipsies," she replied. "The gipsies!" I mocked – "It is only in books that children are stolen by gipsies! You must think of a better story!"

'And now, as if my troubles are not enough, Friday has fallen into one of his mopes. Mopes are what Cruso called them, when without reason Friday would lay down his tools and disappear to some sequestered corner of the island, and then a day later come back and resume his chores as if nothing had intervened. Now he mopes about the passageways or stands at the door, longing to escape, afraid to venture out; or else lies abed and pretends not to hear when I call him. "Friday, Friday," I say, seating myself at his bedside, shaking my head, drifting despite myself into another of the long, issueless colloquies I conduct with him, "how could I have foreseen, when I was carried by the waves on to your island and beheld you with a spear in your hand and the sun shining like a halo behind your head, that our path would take us to a gloomy house in England and a season of empty waiting? Was I wrong to choose Mr Foe? And who is this child he sends us, this mad child? Does he send her as a sign? What is she a sign of?

'"Oh, Friday, how can I make you understand the cravings felt by those of us who live in a world of speech to have our questions answered! It is like our desire, when we kiss someone, to feel the lips we kiss respond to us. Otherwise would we not be content to bestow our kisses on statues, the cold statues of kings and queens and gods and goddesses? Why do you think we do not kiss statues, and sleep with statues in our beds, men with the statues of women and women with the statues of men, statues carved in postures of desire? Do you think it is only because marble is cold? Lie long enough with a statue in your bed, with warm covers over the two of you, and the marble will grow warm. No, it is not because the statue is cold but because it is dead, or rather, because it has never lived and never will.

'"Be assured, Friday, by sitting at your bedside and talking of desire and kisses I do not mean to court you. This is no game in which each word has a second meaning, in which the words say 'Statues are cold' and mean 'Bodies are warm,' or say 'I crave an answer' and mean 'I crave an embrace.' Nor is the denial I now make a false denial of the kind demanded, at least in England (I am ignorant of the customs of your country), by modesty. If I were courting I would court directly, you may be sure. But I am not courting. I am trying to bring it home to you, who have never, for all I know, spoken a word in your life, and certainly never will, what it is to speak into a void, day after day, without answer. And I use a similitude: I say that the desire for answering speech is like the desire for the embrace of, the embrace by, another being. Do I make my meaning clear? You are very likely a virgin, Friday. Perhaps you are even unacquainted with the parts of generation. Yet surely you feel, however obscurely, something within you that draws you toward a woman of your own kind, and not toward an ape or a fish. And what you want to achieve with that woman, though you might puzzle forever over the means were she not to assist you, is what I too want to achieve, and compared in my similitude to an answering kiss.

'"How dismal a fate it would be to go through life unkissed! Yet if you remain in England, Friday, will that not become your fate? Where are you to meet a woman of your own people? We are not a nation rich in slaves. I think of a watch-dog, raised with kindness but kept from birth behind a locked gate. When at last such a dog escapes, the gate having been left open, let us say, the world appears to it so vast, so strange, so full of troubling sights and smells, that it snarls at the first creature to approach, and leaps at its throat, after which it is marked down as vicious, and chained to a post for the rest of its days. I do not say that you are vicious, Friday, I do not say that you will ever be chained, that is not the import of my story. Rather I wish to point to how unnatural a lot it is for a dog or any other creature to be kept from its kind; also to how the impulse of love, which urges us toward our own kind, perishes during confinement, or loses its way. Alas, my stories seem always to have more applications than I intend, so that I must go back and laboriously extract the right application and apologize for the wrong ones and efface them. Some people are born storytellers; I, it would seem, am not.

'"And can we be sure that Mr Foe, whose house this is, whom you have never met, to whom I entrusted the story of the island, did not weeks ago pass away in a hiding-hole in Shoreditch? If so, we shall be forever obscure. His house will be sold under our feet to pay the creditors. There will be no more garden. You will never see Africa. The chill of winter will return, and you will have to wear shoes. Where in England will we find a last broad enough for your feet?

'"Or else I must assume the burden of our story. But what shall I write? You know how dull our life was, in truth. We faced no perils, no ravenous beasts, not even serpents. Food was plentiful, the sun was mild. No pirates landed on our shores, no freebooters, no cannibals save yourself, if you can be called a cannibal. Did Cruso truly believe, I wonder, that you were once a cannibal child? Was it his dark fear that the craving for human flesh would come back to you, that you would one night slit his throat and roast his liver and eat it? Was his talk of cannibals rowing from island to island in search of meat a warning, a masked warning, against you and your appetites? When you

showed your fine white teeth, did Cruso's heart quail?
How I wish you could answer!

'"Yet, all in all, I think the answer must be No.
Surely Cruso must have felt the tedium of life on the
island as keenly in his way as I did in mine, and
perhaps you in yours, and therefore have made up the
roving cannibals to spur himself to vigilance. For the
danger of island life, the danger of which Cruso said
never a word, was the danger of abiding sleep. How
easy it would have been to prolong our slumbers
farther and farther into the hours of daylight till at
last, locked tight in sleep's embrace, we starved to
death (I allude to Cruso and myself, but is the sleeping
sickness not also one of the scourges of Africa?)! Does
it not speak volumes that the first and only piece of
furniture your master fashioned was a bed? How different would it not have been had he built a table and
stool, and extended his ingenuity to the manufacture
of ink and writing-tablets, and then sat down to keep
an authentic journal of his exile day by day, which we
might have brought back to England with us, and
sold to a bookseller, and so saved ourselves this
embroilment with Mr Foe!

'"Alas, we will never make our fortunes, Friday, by
being merely what we are, or were. Think of the spectacle we offer: your master and you on the terraces, I
on the cliffs watching for a sail. Who would wish to
read that there were once two dull fellows on a rock
in the sea who filled their time by digging up stones?
As for me and my yearnings for salvation, one is as
soon sated with yearning as one is with sugar. We
begin to understand why Mr Foe pricked up his ears

when he heard the word *Cannibal*, why he longed for Cruso to have a musket and a carpenter's chest. No doubt he would have preferred Cruso to be younger too, and his sentiments towards me more passionate.

'"But it grows late and there is much to do before nightfall. Are we the only folk in England, I wonder, without lamp or candle? Surely this is an extraordinary existence we lead! For let me assure you, Friday, this is not how Englishmen live. They do not eat carrots morning, noon and night, and live indoors like moles, and go to sleep when the sun sets. Let us only grow rich and I will show you how different living in England can be from living on a rock in the middle of the ocean. Tomorrow, Friday, tomorrow I must settle down to my writing, before the bailiffs come back to expel us, and we have neither carrots to eat nor beds to sleep in.

'"Yet despite what I say, the story of the island was not all tedium and waiting. There were touches of mystery too, were there not?

'"First, the terraces. How many stones did you and your master move? Ten thousand? A hundred thousand? On an island without seed, would you and he not have been as fruitfully occupied in watering the stones where they lay and waiting for them to sprout? If your master had truly wished to be a colonist and leave behind a colony, would he not have been better advised (dare I say this?) to plant his seed in the only womb there was? The farther I journey from his terraces, the less they seem to me like fields waiting to be planted, the more like tombs: those tombs the emperors of Egypt erected for themselves in the desert, in the building of which so many slaves lost their lives. Has that likeness ever occurred to you, Friday; or did news of the emperors of Egypt not reach your part of Africa?

'"Second (I continue to name the mysteries): how did you come to lose your tongue? Your master says the slavers cut it out; but I have never heard of such a practice, nor did I ever meet a slave in Brazil who was dumb. Is the truth that your master cut it out himself and blamed the slavers? If so it was truly an unnatural crime, like chancing upon a stranger and slaying him for no other cause than to keep him from telling the world who slew him. And how would your master have accomplished it? Surely no slave is so slavish as to offer up his parts to the knife. Did Cruso bind you hand and foot and force a block of wood between your teeth and then hack out your tongue? Is that how the act was done? A knife, let us remember, was the sole tool Cruso saved from the wreck. But where did he find the rope with which to bind you? Did he commit the crime while you slept, thrusting his fist into your mouth and cutting out your tongue while you were still befuddled? Or was there some berry native to the island whose juice, smuggled into your food, sent you into a deathlike sleep? Did Cruso cut out your tongue while you were insensible? But how did he staunch the bleeding stump? Why did you not choke on your blood?

'"Unless your tongue was not cut off but merely split, with a cut as neat as a surgeon's, that drew little blood yet made speech ever afterward impossible. Or let us say the sinews that move the tongue were cut and not the tongue itself, the sinews at the base of the tongue. I guess merely, I have not looked into your mouth. When your master asked me to look, I would not. An aversion came over me that we feel for all the mutilated. Why is that so, do you think? Because they put us in mind of what we would rather forget: how easily, at the stroke of a sword or a knife, wholeness and beauty are forever undone? Perhaps. But toward you I felt a deeper revulsion. I could not put out of mind the softness of the tongue, its softness and wetness, and the fact that it does not live in the light; also how helpless it is before the knife, once the barrier of the teeth has been passed. The tongue is like the heart, in that way, is it not? Save that we do not die when a knife pierces the tongue. To that degree we may say the tongue belongs to the world of play, whereas the heart belongs to the world of earnest.

'"Yet it is not the heart but the members of play that elevate us above the beasts: the fingers with which we touch the clavichord or the flute, the tongue with which we jest and lie and seduce. Lacking members of play, what is there left for beasts to do when they are bored but sleep?

'"And then there is the mystery of your submission. Why, during all those years alone with Cruso, did you submit to his rule, when you might easily have slain him, or blinded him and made him into your slave in turn? Is there something in the condition of slavehood that invades the heart and makes a slave a slave for life, as the whiff of ink clings forever to a school-master?

'"Then, if I may be plain – and why may I not be

plain, since talking to you is like talking to the walls?
– why did you not desire me, neither you nor your
master? A woman is cast ashore on your island, a tall
woman with black hair and dark eyes, till a few hours
past the companion of a sea-captain besotted with love
of her. Surely desires kept banked for many years must
have flamed up within you. Why did I not catch you
stealing glances from behind a rock while I bathed?
Do tall women who rise up out of the sea dismay
you? Do they seem like exiled queens come to reclaim
the islands men have stolen from them? But perhaps I
am unjust, perhaps that is a question for Cruso alone;
for what have you ever stolen in your life, you who
are yourself stolen? Nevertheless, did Cruso in his way
and do you in your way believe I came to claim
dominion over you, and is that why you were wary of
me?

'"I ask these questions because they are the questions any reader of our story will ask. I had no
thought, when I was washed ashore, of becoming a
castaway's wife. But the reader is bound to ask why it
was that, in all the nights I shared your master's hut,
he and I did not come together more than once as
man and woman do. Is the answer that our island was
not a garden of desire, like that in which our first
parents went naked, and coupled as innocently as
beasts? I believe your master would have had it be a
garden of labour; but, lacking a worthy object for his
labours, descended to carrying stones, as ants carry
grains of sand to and fro for want of better occupation.

'"And then there is the final mystery: What were

you about when you paddled out to sea upon your log and scattered petals on the water? I will tell you what I have concluded: that you scattered the petals over the place where your ship went down, and scattered them in memory of some person who perished in the wreck, perhaps a father or a mother or a sister or a brother, or perhaps a whole family, or perhaps a dear friend. On the sorrows of Friday, I once thought to tell Mr Foe, but did not, a story entire of itself might be built; whereas from the indifference of Cruso there is little to be squeezed.

'"I must go, Friday. You thought that carrying stones was the hardest of labours. But when you see me at Mr Foe's desk making marks with the quill, think of each mark as a stone, and think of the paper as the island, and imagine that I must disperse the stones over the face of the island, and when that is done and the taskmaster is not satisfied (was Cruso ever satisfied with your labours?) must pick them up again (which, in the figure, is scoring out the marks) and dispose them according to another scheme, and so forth, day after day; all of this because Mr Foe has run away from his debts. Sometimes I believe it is I who have become the slave. No doubt you would smile, if you could understand."'

*   *

'Days pass. Nothing changes. We hear no word from you, and the townsfolk pay us no more heed than if we were ghosts. I have been once to Dalston market, taking a tablecloth and a case of spoons, which I sold to buy necessaries. Otherwise we exist by the produce of your garden.

'The girl has resumed her station at the gate. I try to ignore her.

'Writing proves a slow business. After the flurry of the mutiny and the death of the Portuguese captain, after I have met Cruso and come to know somewhat of the life he leads, what is there to say? There was too little desire in Cruso and Friday: too little desire to escape, too little desire for a new life. Without desire how is it possible to make a story? It was an island of sloth, despite the terracing. I ask myself what past historians of the castaway state have done – whether in despair they have not begun to make up lies.

'Yet I persevere. A painter engaged to paint a dull scene – let us say two men digging in a field – has means at hand to lend allure to his subject. He can set the golden hues of the first man's skin against the sooty hues of the second's, creating a play of light against dark. By artfully representing their attitudes he can indicate which is master, which slave. And to render his composition more lively he is at liberty to bring into it what may not be there on the day he paints but may be there on other days, such as a pair of gulls wheeling overhead, the beak of one parted in a cry, and in one corner, upon a faraway crag, a band of apes.

'Thus we see the painter selecting and composing and rendering particulars in order to body forth a pleasing fullness in his scene. The storyteller, by contrast (forgive me, I would not lecture you on storytelling if you were here in the flesh!), must divine which episodes of his history hold promise of fullness, and tease from them their hidden meanings, braiding these together as one braids a rope.

'Teasing and braiding can, like any craft, be learned. But as to determining which episodes hold promise (as oysters hold pearls), it is not without justice that this art is called divining. Here the writer can of himself effect nothing: he must wait on the grace of illumination. Had I known, on the island, that it would one day fall to me to be our storyteller, I would have been more zealous to interrogate Cruso. "Cast your thoughts back, Cruso," I would have said, as I lay beside him in the dark – "Can you recall no moment at which the purpose of our life here has been all at once illuminated? As you have walked on the hillsides or clambered on the cliffs in quest of eggs, have you never been struck of a sudden by the living, breathing quality of this island, as if it were some great beast from before the Flood that has slept through the centuries insensible of the insects scurrying on its back, scratching an existence for themselves? Are we insects, Cruso, in the greater view? Are we no better than the ants?" Or when he lay dying on the [H] *obart* I might have said: "Cruso, you are leaving us behind, you are going where we cannot follow you. Is there no last word you wish to speak, from the vantage of one departing? Is there not something you wish to confess?"'

*   *

'We trudge through the forest, the girl and I. It is

autumn, we have taken the coach to Epping, now we are making our way to Cheshunt, though leaves lie so thick underfoot, gold and brown and red, that I cannot be sure we have not strayed from the path.

'The girl is behind me. "Where are you taking me?" she asks for the hundredth time. "I am taking you to see your real mother," I reply. "I know who is my real mother," she says – "You are my real mother." "You will know your true mother when you see her," I reply – "Walk faster, we must be back before nightfall." She trots to keep pace with me.

'Deeper into the forest we go, miles from human habitation. "Let us rest," I say. Side by side we seat ourselves against the trunk of a great oak. From her basket she brings forth bread and cheese and a flask of water. We eat and drink.

'We plod on. Have we lost our way? She keeps falling behind. "We will never be back before dark," she complains. "You must trust me," I reply.

'In the darkest heart of the forest I halt. "Let us rest again," I say. I take her cloak from her and spread it over the leaves. We sit. "Come to me," I say, and put an arm around her. A light trembling runs through her body. It is the second time I have allowed her to touch me. "Close your eyes," I say. It is so quiet that we can hear the brushing of our clothes, the grey stuff of hers against the black stuff of mine. Her head lies on my shoulder. In a sea of fallen leaves we sit, she and I, two substantial beings.

'"I have brought you here to tell you of your parentage," I commence. "I do not know who told you that your father was a brewer from Deptford who fled to the Low Countries, but the story is false. Your father is a man named Daniel Foe. He is the man who set you to watching the house in Newington. Just as it was he who told you I am your mother, I will vouch he is the author of the story of the brewer. He maintains whole regiments in Flanders."

'She makes to speak, but I hush her.

'"I know you will say it is not true," I continue. "I know you will say you have never met this Daniel Foe. But ask yourself: by what agency did the news reach you that your true mother was one Susan Barton who lived at such and such a house in Stoke Newington?"

'"My name is Susan Barton," she whispers.

'"That is small proof. You will find many Susan Bartons in this kingdom, if you are willing to hunt them down. I repeat: what you know of your parentage comes to you in the form of stories, and the stories have but a single source."

'"Who is my true mother then?" she says.

'"You are father-born. You have no mother. The pain you feel is the pain of lack, not the pain of loss. What you hope to regain in my person you have in truth never had."

'"Father-born," she says – "It is a word I have never heard before." She shakes her head.

'What do I mean by it, father-born? I wake in the grey of a London dawn with the word still faintly in my ears. The street is empty, I observe from the window. Is the girl gone forever? Have I expelled her, banished her, lost her at last in the forest? Will she sit by the oak tree till the falling leaves cover her, her and her basket, and nothing is left to meet the eye but a field of browns and golds?'

*   *

'Dear Mr Foe,

'Some days ago Friday discovered your robes (the robes in the wardrobe, that is) and your wigs. Are they the robes of a guild-master? I did not know there was a guild of authors.

'The robes have set him dancing, which I had never seen him do before. In the mornings he dances in the kitchen, where the windows face east. If the sun is shining he does his dance in a patch of sunlight, holding out his arms and spinning in a circle, his eyes shut, hour after hour, never growing fatigued or dizzy. In the afternoon he removes himself to the drawing-room, where the window faces west, and does his dancing there.

'In the grip of the dancing he is not himself. He is beyond human reach. I call his name and am ignored, I put out a hand and am brushed aside. All the while he dances he makes a humming noise in his throat, deeper than his usual voice; sometimes he seems to be singing.

'For myself I do not care how much he sings and dances so long as he carries out his few duties. For I will not delve while he spins. Last night I decided I would take the robe away from him, to bring him to his senses. However, when I stole into his room he was awake, his hands already gripping the robe, which was spread over the bed, as though he read my thoughts. So I retreated.

'Friday and his dancing: I may bemoan the tedium of life in your house, but there is never a lack of things to write of. It is as though animalcules of words lie dissolved in your ink-well, ready to be dipped up and flow from the pen and take form on the paper. From downstairs to upstairs, from house to island, from the girl to Friday: it seems necessary only to establish the poles, the here and the there, the now and the then – after that the words of themselves do the journeying. I had not guessed it was so easy to be an author.

'You will find the house very bare on your return. First the bailiffs plundered it (I cannot use a kinder term), and now I too have been taking odds and ends (I keep an inventory, you have only to ask and I will send it). Unhappily I am forced to sell in the quarters where thieves sell, and to accept the prices thieves receive. On my excursions I wear a black dress and bonnet I found upstairs in the trunk with the initials M.J. on the lid (who is M.J.?). In this garb I become older than my years: as I picture myself, a widow of forty in straitened circumstances. Yet despite my precautions I lie awake at night picturing how I might be seized by some rapacious shopkeeper and held for the constables, till I am forced to give away your candlesticks as a bribe for my freedom.

'Last week I sold the one mirror not taken by the bailiffs, the little mirror with the gilt frame that stood on your cabinet. Dare I confess I am happy it is gone? How I have aged! In Bahia the sallow Portuguese women would not believe I had a grown daughter. But life with Cruso put lines on my brow, and the house of Foe has only deepened them. Is your house a house of sleepers, like the cave where men close their eyes in one reign and wake in another with long white beards? Brazil seems as far away as the age of Arthur. Is it possible I have a daughter there, growing farther from me every day, as I from her? Do the clocks of Brazil run at the same pace as ours? While I grow old, does she remain forever young? And how has it come about that in the day of the twopenny post I share a house with a man from the darkest times of barbarism? So many questions!'

*   *

'Dear Mr Foe,

'I am growing to understand why you wanted Cruso to have a musket and be besieged by cannibals. I thought it was a sign you had no regard for the truth. I forgot you are a writer who knows above all how many words can be sucked from a cannibal feast, how few from a woman cowering from the wind. It is all a matter of words and the number of words, is it not?

'Friday sits at table in his wig and robes and eats pease pudding. I ask myself: Did human flesh once pass those lips? Truly, cannibals are terrible; but most terrible of all is to think of the little cannibal children, their eyes closing in pleasure as they chew the tasty fat of their neighbours. I shiver. For surely eating human flesh is like falling into sin: having fallen once you discover in yourself a taste for it, and fall all the more readily thereafter. I shiver as I watch Friday dancing in the kitchen, with his robes whirling about him and the wig flapping on his head, and his eyes shut and his thoughts far away, not on the island, you may be sure, not on the pleasures of digging and carrying, but on the time before, when he was a savage among savages. Is it not only a matter of time before the new Friday whom Cruso created is sloughed off and the old Friday of the cannibal forests returns? Have I misjudged Cruso all this time: was it to punish him for his sins that he cut out Friday's tongue? Better had he drawn his teeth instead!'

* *

'Searching through a chest of drawers some days ago for items to take to market, I came across a case of recorders you must once have played: perhaps you played the big bass recorder while your sons and daughters played the smaller ones. (What has happened to your sons and daughters? Could they not be trusted to shelter you from the law?) I took out the smallest of these, the soprano, and set it aside where Friday would find it. The next morning I heard him toying with it; soon he had so far mastered it as to play the tune of six notes I will forever associate with the island and Cruso's first sickness. This he played over and over all morning. When I came to remonstrate, I found him spinning slowly around with the flute to his lips and his eyes shut; he paid no heed to me, perhaps not even hearing my words. How like a savage to master a strange instrument – to the extent that he is able without a tongue – and then be content forever to play one tune upon it! It is a form of in-curiosity, is it not, a form of sloth. But I digress.

'While I was polishing the bass flute, and idly blowing a few notes upon it, it occurred to me that if there were any language accessible to Friday, it would be the language of music. So I closed the door and practised the blowing and the fingering as I had seen people do, till I could play Friday's little tune tolerably well, and one or two others, to my ear more melodious. All the while I was playing, which I did in the dark, to spare the candle, Friday lay awake downstairs in his own dark listening to the deeper tones of my flute, the like of which he could never have heard before.

'When Friday commenced his dancing and fluteplaying this morning, I was ready: I sat upstairs on my bed, my legs crossed, and played Friday's tune, first in unison with him, then in the intervals when he was not playing; and went on playing as long as he did, till my hands ached and my head reeled. The music we made was not pleasing: there was a subtle discord all the time, though we seemed to be playing the same notes. Yet our instruments were made to play together, else why were they in the same case?

'When Friday fell silent awhile, I came downstairs to the kitchen. "So, Friday," I said, and smiled — "we are become musicians together." And I raised my flute and blew his tune again, till a kind of contentment came over me. I thought: It is true, I am not conversing with Friday, but is this not as good? Is conversation not simply a species of music in which first the one takes up the refrain and then the other? Does it matter what the refrain of our conversation is any more than it matters what tune it is we play? And I asked myself further: Are not both music and conversation like love? Who would venture to say that what passes between lovers is of substance (I refer to their lovemaking, not their talk), yet is it not true that something is passed between them, back and forth, and they come away refreshed and healed for a while of their loneliness? As long as I have music in common with Friday, perhaps he and I will need no language. And if there had been music on our island, if Friday and I had filled the evening with melody, perchance – who can say? – Cruso might at last have relented, and picked up the third pipe, and learned to finger it, if his fingers had not by then been too stiff, and the three of us might have become a consort (from which you may conclude, Mr Foe, that what we needed from the wreck was not a chest of tools but a case of flutes).

'For that hour in your kitchen I believe I was at ease with the life that has befallen me.

'But alas, just as we cannot exchange forever the same utterances – "Good day, sir" – "Good day" – and believe we are conversing, or perform forever the same motion and call it lovemaking, so it is with music: we cannot forever play the same tune and be content. Or so at least it is with civilized people. Thus at last I could not restrain myself from varying the tune, first making one note into two half-notes, then changing two of the notes entirely, turning it into a new tune and a pretty one too, so fresh to my ear that I was sure Friday would follow me. But no, Friday persisted in the old tune, and the two tunes played together formed no pleasing counterpoint, but on the contrary jangled and jarred. Did Friday in truth so much as hear me, I began to wonder? I ceased playing, and his eyes (which were always closed when he did his flute-playing and spinning) did not open; I blew long blasts and the lids did not so much as flutter. So now I knew that all the time I had stood there playing to Friday's dancing, thinking he and I made a consort, he had been insensible of me. And indeed, when I stepped forward in some pique and grasped at him to halt the infernal spinning, he seemed to feel my touch no more than if it had been a fly's; from which I concluded that he was in a trance of possession, and his soul more in Africa than in Newington. Tears came to my eyes, I am ashamed to say; all the elation of my discovery that through the medium of music I might at last converse with Friday was dashed, and bitterly I began to recognize that it might not be mere dullness that kept him shut up in himself, nor the accident of the loss of his tongue, nor even an incapacity to distinguish speech from babbling, but a disdain for intercourse with me. Watching him whirling in his dance, I had to hold back an urge to strike him and tear the wig and robes away and thus rudely teach him he was not alone on this earth.

'Had I struck Friday, I now ask myself, would he have borne the blow meekly? Cruso never chastised him that I saw. Had the cutting out of his tongue taught him eternal obedience, or at least the outward form of obedience, as gelding takes the fire out of a stallion?'

*   *

'Dear Mr Foe,

'I have written a deed granting Friday his freedom and signed it in Cruso's name. This I have sewn into a little bag and hung on a cord around Friday's neck.

'If Friday is not mine to set free, whose is he? No man can be the slave of a dead hand. If Cruso had a widow, I am she; if there are two widows, I am the first. What life do I live but that of Cruso's widow? On Cruso's island I was washed ashore; from that all else has flowed. I am the woman washed ashore.

'I write from on the road. We are on the road to Bristol. The sun is shining. I walk ahead, Friday follows carrying the pack which contains our provisions as well as some few items from the house, and the wig, from which he will not be parted. The robes he wears, instead of a coat.

'No doubt we make a strange sight, the barefoot woman in breeches and her black slave (my shoes pinch, the old apeskin sandals are fallen apart). When passers-by stop to question us, I say that I am on my way to my brother in Slough, that my footman and I were robbed of our horses and clothes and valuables by highwaymen. This story earns me curious looks. Why? Are there no more highwaymen on the roads? Were all the highwaymen hanged while I was in Bahia? Do I seem an unlikely owner of horses and valuables? Or is my air too blithe to befit one stripped bare mere hours before?

*   *

'In Ealing we passed a cobbler's. I took out one of the books from the pack, a volume of sermons handsomely bound in calf, and offered to exchange it for new shoes. The cobbler pointed to your name on the flyleaf. "Mr Foe of Stoke Newington," I said, "lately deceased." "Have you no other books?" asked he. I offered him the *Pilgrimages* of Purchas, the first volume, and for that he gave me a pair of shoes, stoutly made and well-fitting. You will protest that he gained by the exchange. But a time comes when there are more important things than books. "Who is the blackfellow?" the cobbler asked. "He is a slave who is now free, that I am taking to Bristol to find him a passage back to his own people." "It is a long road to Bristol," said the cobbler – "Does he speak English?" "He understands some things but he does not speak," I replied. A hundred miles and more to Bristol: how many more questioners, how many more questions? What a boon to be stricken speechless too!

'To you, Mr Foe, a journey to Bristol may call to mind hearty meals at roadside inns and diverting encounters with strangers from all walks of life. But remember, a woman alone must travel like a hare, one ear forever cocked for the hounds. If it happens we are set upon by footpads, what protection will Friday afford me? He never had call to protect Cruso; indeed, his upbringing has taught him to not so much as raise a hand in self-defence. Why should he regard an assault on me as of concern to him? He does not understand that I am leading him to freedom. He does not know what freedom is. Freedom is a word, less than a word, a noise, one of the multitude of noises I make when I open my mouth. His master is dead, now he has a mistress – that is all he knows. Having never wished for a master, why should he guard his mistress? How can he guess that there is any goal to our rambling, that without me he is lost? "Bristol is a great port," I tell him. "Bristol is where we landed when the ship brought us back from the island. Bristol is where you saw the great chimney belching smoke, that so amazed you. From Bristol ships sail to all corners of the globe, principally to the Americas, but also to Africa, which was once your home. In Bristol we will seek out a ship to take you back to the land of your birth, or else to Brazil and the life of a freeman there."'

*   *

'Yesterday the worst came to pass. We were stopped on the Windsor road by two drunken soldiers who made their intention on my person all too plain. I broke away and took to the fields and escaped, with Friday at my heels, in mortal terror all the while we ran that they would shoot upon us. Now I pin my hair up under my hat and wear a coat at all times, hoping to pass for a man.

'In the afternoon it began to rain. We sheltered under a hedge, trusting it was but a shower. But the rain had truly set in. So at last we trudged on, wet to the bone, till we came to an alehouse. With some misgiving I pushed the door open and led Friday in, making for a table in the obscurest corner.

'I do not know whether the people of that place had never seen a black man before, or never seen a woman in breeches, or simply never seen such a be-draggled pair, but all speech died as we entered, and we crossed the room in a silence in which I could plainly hear the splashing of water from the eaves outside. I thought to myself: This is a great mistake – better we had sought out a hayrick and sheltered there, hungry or not. But I put on a bold face and pulled out a chair for Friday, indicating to him that he should sit. From under the sodden robe came the same smell I had smelled when the sailors brought him aboard ship: a smell of fear.

'The innkeeper himself came to our table. I asked civilly for two measures of small beer and a plate of bread and cheese. He made no reply, but stared pointedly at Friday and then at me. "This is my manservant," I said – "He is as clean as you or I." "Clean or dirty, he wears shoes in this house," he replied. I coloured. "If you will attend to serving us, I will attend to my servant's dress," I said. "This is a clean house, we do not serve strollers or gipsies," said the innkeeper, and turned his back on us. As we made our way to the door a lout stuck out his foot, causing Friday to stumble, at which there was much guf-fawing.

'We skulked under hedgerows till darkness fell and then crept into a barn. I was shivering by this time in my wet clothes. Feeling about in the dark, I came to a crib filled with clean hay. I stripped off my clothes and burrowed like a mole into the hay, but still found no warmth. So I climbed out again and donned the sodden clothes and stood miserably in the dark, my teeth chattering. Friday seemed to have disappeared. I could not even hear his breathing. As a man born in the tropic forest he should have felt the cold more keenly than I; yet he walked barefoot in the dead of winter and did not complain. "Friday," I whispered. There was no reply.

'In some despair, and not knowing what else to do, I stretched out my arms and, with my head thrown back, began to turn in Friday's dance. It is a way of drying my clothes, I told myself: I dry them by creating a breeze. It is a way of keeping warm. Otherwise I shall perish of cold. I felt my jaw relax, and heat, or the illusion of heat, begin to steal through my limbs. I danced till the very straw seemed to warm under my feet. I have discovered why Friday dances in England, I thought, smiling to myself; which, if we had remained at Mr Foe's, I should never have learned. And I should never have made this discovery had I not been soaked to the skin and then set down in the dark in an empty barn. From which we may infer that there is after all design in our lives, and if we wait long enough we are bound to see that design unfolding; just as, observing a carpet-maker, we may see at first glance only a tangle of threads; yet, if we are patient, flowers begin to emerge under our gaze, and prancing unicorns, and turrets.

'Thinking these thoughts, spinning round, my eyes closed, a smile on my lips, I fell, I believe, into a kind of trance; for when next I knew, I was standing still, breathing heavily, with somewhere at my mind's edge an intimation that I had been far away, that I had seen wondrous sights. Where am I? I asked myself, and crouched down and stroked the floor; and when it came back to me that I was in Berkshire, a great pang wrenched my heart; for what I had seen in my trance, whatever it had been – I could summon back nothing distinct, yet felt a glow of after-memory, if you can understand that – had been a message (but from whom?) to tell me there were other lives open to me than this one in which I trudged with Friday across the English countryside, a life of which I was already heartily sick. And in that same instant I understood why Friday had danced all day in your house: it was to remove himself, or his spirit, from Newington and England, and from me too. For was it to be wondered at that Friday found life with me as burdensome as I found life with him? As long as we two are cast in each other's company, I thought, perhaps it is best that we dance and spin and transport ourselves. "It is your turn to dance, Friday," I called into the darkness, and climbed into my crib and piled hay upon myself and fell asleep.

'At first light I awoke, glowing with warmth, calm and refreshed. I discovered Friday asleep on a hurdle behind the door and shook him, surprised to find him so sluggish, for I had thought savages slept with one eye open. But likely he had lost his savage habits on the island, where he and Cruso had no enemies.'

*   *

'I do not wish to make our journey to Bristol seem more full of incident than it has truly been. But I must tell you of the dead babe.

'Some miles outside Marlborough, as we were

walking steadily enough down an empty road, my eye fell on a parcel lying in the ditch. I sent Friday to fetch it, thinking I know not what, perhaps that it was a bundle of clothes fallen from a carriage; or perhaps I was simply curious. But when I began to unwind the wrapping-cloth I found it to be bloody, and was afraid to go on. Yet where there is blood there is fascination. So I went on and unwrapped the body, stillborn or perhaps stifled, all bloody with the afterbirth, of a little girl, perfectly formed, her hands clenched up by her ears, her features peaceful, barely an hour or two in the world. Whose child was she? The fields around us were empty. Half a mile away stood a cluster of cottages; but how welcome would we be if, like accusers, we returned to their doorstep that which they had cast out? Or what if they took the child to be mine and laid hands on me and haled me before the magistrates? So I wrapped the babe again in its bloody winding-cloth and laid it in the bottom of the ditch and guiltily led Friday away from that place. Try though I might, I could not put from my thoughts the little sleeper who would never awake, the pinched eyes that would never see the sky, the curled fingers that would never open. Who was the child but I, in another life? Friday and I slept among a grove of trees that night (it was the night I tried to eat acorns, I was so hungry). I had slept but a minute when I awoke with a start thinking I must go back to where the child was hid before the crows got to her, the crows and the rats; and, before I gathered my wits, had even stumbled to my feet. I lay down again with my coat pulled over my ears and tears coursing down my cheeks. My thoughts ran to Friday, I could not stop them, it was an effect of the hunger. Had I not been there to restrain him, would he in his hunger have eaten the babe? I told myself I did him wrong to think of him as a cannibal or worse, a devourer of the dead. But Cruso had planted the seed in my mind, and now I could not look on Friday's lips without calling to mind what meat must once have passed them.

'I grant without reserve that in such thinking lie the seeds of madness. We cannot shrink in disgust from our neighbour's touch because his hands, that are clean now, were once dirty. We must cultivate, all of us, a certain ignorance, a certain blindness, or society will not be tolerable. If Friday forswore human flesh during his fifteen years on the island, why should I not believe he had forsworn it forever? And if in his heart of hearts he remained a cannibal, would a warm living woman not make a better meal than the cold stiff corpse of a child? The blood hammered in my ears; the creak of a branch, or a cloud passing across the moon, made me think Friday was upon me; though part of me knew he was the same dull blackfellow as ever, another part, over which I had no mastery, insisted on his bloodlust. So I slept not a wink, till the light paled and I saw Friday dead asleep a few paces away, his horny feet that seemed never to feel the cold sticking out from under his robe.'

*   *

'Though we walk in silence, there is a buzz of words in my head, all addressed to you. In the dark days of

Newington I believed you were dead: you had starved in your lodgings and been given a pauper's burial; you had been hunted down and committed to the Fleet, to perish of misery and neglect. But now a stronger certainty has come over me, which I cannot explain. You are alive and well, and as we march down the Bristol road I talk to you as if you were beside me, my familiar ghost, my companion. Cruso too. There are times when Cruso comes back to me, morose as ever he was in the old days (which I can bear).'

*   *

'Arriving in Marlborough, I found a stationer's and for half a guinea sold him Pakenham's *Travels in Abyssinia*, in quarto, from your library. Though glad to be relieved of so heavy a book, I was sorry too, for I had no time to read in it and learn more of Africa, and so be of greater assistance to Friday in regaining his homeland. Friday is not from Abyssinia, I know. But on the road to Abyssinia the traveller must pass through many kingdoms: why should Friday's kingdom not be one of these?

'The weather remaining fine, Friday and I sleep under hedgerows. For prudence sake we lie low, for we make an irregular couple. "Are you his mistress?" asked an old man of us, as we sat on the church steps yesterday eating our bread. Was it a saucy question? The fellow seemed in earnest. "He is a slave whose master set him free on his deathbed," I replied — "I accompany him to Bristol, where he will take ship for Africa and his native land." "So you are returning to

Africa," said the old man, turning to Friday. "He has no speech," I put in – "He lost his tongue as a child, now he speaks only in gestures. In gestures and actions." "You will have many stories to tell them in Africa, will you not?" said the old fellow, speaking louder, as we do to deaf people. Friday regarded him emptily, but he would not be deterred. "You have seen many sights, I am sure," he continued – "great cities, ships as big as castles. You will not be believed when you relate all you have seen." "He has lost his tongue, there is no language in which he can speak, not even his own," said I, hoping the fellow would go away. But perhaps he too was deaf. "Are you gipsies then?" said he – "Are you gipsies, you and he?" For a moment I was lost for words. "He has been a slave, now he is returning to Africa," I repeated. "Aye," he said, "but we call them gipsies when they roam about with their dirty faces, men and women all higgledy-piggledy together, looking for mischief." And he got to his feet and faced me, propped on his stick, as though daring me to gainsay him. "Come, Friday," I murmured, and we left the square.

'I am amused now to think of this skirmish, but then I was shaken. Living like a mole in your house has quite taken away my nut-brown island hue; but it is true, on the road I have barely washed, feeling none the worse for it. I remember a shipload of gipsies, dark and mistrustful folk, cast out of Galicia in Spain, stepping ashore in Bahia on to a strange continent. Twice have Friday and I been called gipsies. What is a gipsy? What is a highwayman? Words seem to have new meanings here in the west country. Am I become a gipsy unknown to myself?'

*   *

'Yesterday we arrived in Bristol and made directly for the docks, which Friday showed every sign of recognizing. There I stopped every seaman who passed, asking whether he knew of a ship sailing for Africa or the East. At last we were directed toward an Indiaman standing out on the road, due to sail for Trincomalee and the spice islands. By great good fortune a lighter just then berthed that had been conveying stores to it, and the first mate stepped ashore. Asking his pardon for our travel-stained appearance, assuring him we were not gipsies, I presented Friday as a former slave from the Americas, happily now free, who wished to make his way home to Africa. Regrettably, I went on, Friday was master of neither English nor any other language, having lost his tongue to the slave-catchers. But he was diligent and obedient and asked for no more than to work his passage to Africa as a deck-hand.

'At this the mate smiled. "Africa is a great place, madam, greater than I can tell you," he said. "Does your man know where he wishes to be set down? He may be put ashore in Africa and still be farther from his home than from here to Muscovy."

'I shrugged off his question. "When the time comes I am convinced he will know," I said – "Our feeling for home is never lost. Will you take him or no?" "Has he ever sailed before?" asked the mate. "He has sailed and been shipwrecked too," I replied – "He is a mariner of long standing."

'So the mate consented to take us to the master of the Indiaman. We followed him to a coffee-house, where the master sat huddled with two merchants. After a long wait we were presented to him. Again I related the story of Friday and his desire to return to Africa. "Have you been to Africa, madam?" asked the captain. "No, sir, I have not," I replied, "but that is neither here nor there." "And you will not be accompanying your man?" "I will not." "Then let me tell you," said he: "One half of Africa is desert and the rest a stinking fever-ridden forest. Your blackfellow would be better off in England. Nevertheless, if he is set on it, I will take him." At which my heart leapt. "Have you his papers of manumission?" he asked. I motioned to Friday (who had stood like a stick through these exchanges, understanding nothing) that I wished to open the bag about his neck, and showed the captain the paper signed in Cruso's name, which seemed to please him. "Very well," said he, pocketing the paper, "we will put your man ashore wherever in Africa he instructs us. But now you must say your farewells: we sail in the morning."

'Whether it was the captain's manner or whether the glance I caught passing between him and the mate I cannot say, but suddenly I knew all was not as it seemed to be. "The paper is Friday's," I said, holding out my hand to receive it – "It is his only proof that he is a free man." And when the captain had returned the paper to me, I added: "Friday cannot come aboard now, for he has belongings to fetch from our rooms in the city." By which they guessed I had seen through their scheme (which was to sell Friday into slavery a second time): the captain shrugged his shoulders and turned his back to me, and that was the end of that.

'So the castle I had built in the air, namely that Friday should sail for Africa and I return to London my own mistress at last, came tumbling about my ears. Where a ship's-master was honest, I discovered, he would not accept so unpromising a deck-hand as Friday. Only the more unscrupulous – of whom I met a host in the days that followed – pretended to welcome us, seeing me, no doubt, as an easy dupe and Friday as their God-sent prey. One of these claimed to be sailing for Calicut, making port at the Cape of Good Hope on the way, where he promised to set Friday ashore; while his true destination, as I learned from the wharfmaster, was Jamaica.

'Was I too suspicious? All I know is, I would not sleep easy tonight if Friday were on the high seas destined a second time, all unwittingly, for the plantations. A woman may bear a child she does not want, and rear it without loving it, yet be ready to defend it with her life. Thus it has become, in a manner of speaking, between Friday and myself. I do not love him, but he is mine. That is why he remains in England. That is why he is here.'

III

The staircase was dark and mean. My knock echoed as if on emptiness. But I knocked a second time, and heard a shuffling, and from behind the door a voice, his voice, low and cautious. 'It is I, Susan Barton,' I announced – 'I am alone, with Friday.' Whereupon the door opened and he stood before me, the same Foe I had first set eyes on in Kensington Row, but leaner and quicker, as though vigilance and a spare diet agreed with him.

'May we come in?' I said.

He made way and we entered his refuge. The room was lit by a single window, through which poured the afternoon sun. The view was to the north, over the roofs of Whitechapel. For furniture there was a table and chair, and a bed, slovenly made; one corner of the room was curtained off.

'It is not as I imagined it,' I said. 'I expected dust thick on the floor, and gloom. But life is never as we expect it to be. I recall an author reflecting that after death we may find ourselves not among choirs of angels but in some quite ordinary place, as for instance a bath-house on a hot afternoon, with spiders dozing in the corners; at the time it will seem like any Sunday in the country; only later will it come home to us that we are in eternity.'

'It is an author I have not read.'

'The idea has remained with me from my childhood. But I have come to ask about another story. The history of ourselves and the island – how does it progress? Is it written?'

'It progresses, but progresses slowly, Susan. It is a slow story, a slow history. How did you find your way to me?'

'By good fortune entirely. I met your old house-keeper Mrs Thrush in Covent Garden after Friday and I came back from Bristol (I wrote you letters on the Bristol road, I have them with me, I will give them to you). Mrs Thrush directed us to the boy who runs errands for you, with a token that we were to be trusted, and he led us to this house.'

'It is excellent that you have come, for there is more I must know about Bahia, that only you can tell me.'

'Bahia is not part of my story,' I replied, 'but let me tell you whatever I can. Bahia is a city built on hills. To convey cargoes from the harbour to their ware-houses, the merchants have therefore spanned a great cable, with pulleys and windlasses. From the streets you see bales of cargo sail overhead on the cable all day. The streets are a-bustle with people going about their business, slave and free, Portuguese and Negro and Indian and half-breed. But the Portuguese women are seldom to be seen abroad. For the Portuguese are a very jealous race. They have a saying: In her life a woman has but three occasions to leave the house – for her baptism, her wedding, and her burial. A woman who goes abroad freely is thought a whore. I was thought a whore. But there are so many whores there, or, as I prefer to call them, free women, that I was not daunted. In the cool of the evening the free women of Bahia don their finest clothes, put hoops of gold about their necks and golden bracelets on their arms and ornaments of gold in their hair, and walk the streets; for gold is cheap there. The most handsome are the women of colour, or *mulatas* as they are called. The Crown has failed to halt the private traffic in gold, which is mined in the interior and sold by the miners to the goldsmiths. Alas, I have nothing to show you of the craft of these excellent smiths, not even a pin. All I had was taken from me by the mutineers. I came ashore on the island with nothing but the clothes I wore, red as a beetroot from the sun, my hands raw and blistered. It is no wonder I failed to charm Cruso.'

'And Friday?'

'Friday?'

'Did Friday ever grow enamoured of you?'

'How are we ever to know what goes on in the heart of Friday? But I think not.' I turned to Friday, who had been squatting all the while by the door with his head on his knees. 'Do you love me, Friday?' I called softly. Friday did not so much as raise his head. 'We have lived too close for love, Mr Foe. Friday has grown to be my shadow. Do our shadows love us, for all that they are never parted from us?'

Foe smiled. 'Tell me more of Bahia,' he said.

'There is much to be said of Bahia. Bahia is a world in itself. But why? Bahia is not the island. Bahia was but a stepping stone on my way.'

'That may not be so,' replied Foe cautiously. 'Rehearse your story and you will see. The story begins in London. Your daughter is abducted or elopes, I do not know which, it does not matter. In quest of her you sail to Bahia, for you have intelligence that she is there. In Bahia you spend no less than two years, two fruitless years. How do you live all this time? How do you clothe yourself? Where do you sleep? How do you pass the days? Who are your friends? These are questions that are asked, which we must answer. And what has been the fate of your daughter? Even in the great spaces of Brazil a daughter does not vanish like smoke. Is it possible that while you are seeking her she is seeking you? But enough of questions. At last you despair. You abandon your quest and depart. Shortly thereafter your daughter arrives in Bahia, from the backlands, in search of you. She hears talk of a tall Englishwoman who has taken ship for Lisbon, and follows. She haunts the docks of Lisbon and Oporto. Rough sailors think her a blessed simpleton and treat her with kindness. But no one has heard of a tall Englishwoman off a ship from Bahia. Are you on the Azores, gazing out to sea, mourning, like Ariadne? We do not know. Time passes. Your daughter despairs. Then chance brings to her ears the story of a woman rescued from an island where she has been marooned with an old man and his black slave. Is this woman by some chance her mother? She follows a trail of rumour from Bristol to London, to the house where the woman had briefly taken service (this is the house on Kensington Row). There she learns the woman's name. It is the same as hers.

'We therefore have five parts in all: the loss of the daughter; the quest for the daughter in Brazil; abandonment of the quest, and the adventure of the island; assumption of the quest by the daughter; and reunion of the daughter with her mother. It is thus that we make up a book: loss, then quest, then recovery; beginning, then middle, then end. As to novelty, this is lent by the island episode – which is properly the second part of the middle – and by the reversal in which the daughter takes up the quest abandoned by her mother.'

All the joy I had felt in finding my way to Foe fled me. I sat heavy-limbed.

'The island is not a story in itself,' said Foe gently, laying a hand on my knee. 'We can bring it to life only by setting it within a larger story. By itself it is no better than a waterlogged boat drifting day after day in an empty ocean till one day, humbly and without commotion, it sinks. The island lacks light and shade. It is too much the same throughout. It is like a loaf of bread. It will keep us alive, certainly, if we are starved of reading; but who will prefer it when there are tastier confections and pastries to be had?'

'In the letters you did not read,' I said, 'I told you of my conviction that, if the story seems stupid, that is only because it so doggedly holds its silence. The shadow whose lack you feel is there: it is the loss of Friday's tongue.'

117

Foe made no reply, and I went on. 'The story of Friday's tongue is a story unable to be told, or unable to be told by me. That is to say, many stories can be told of Friday's tongue, but the true story is buried within Friday, who is mute. The true story will not be heard till by art we have found a means of giving voice to Friday.

'Mr Foe,' I proceeded, speaking with gathering difficulty, 'when I lived in your house I would sometimes lie awake upstairs listening to the pulse of blood in my ears and to the silence from Friday below, a silence that rose up the stairway like smoke, like a welling of black smoke. Before long I could not breathe, I would feel I was stifling in my bed. My lungs, my heart, my head were full of black smoke. I had to spring up and open the curtains and put my head outside and breathe fresh air and see for myself that there were stars still in the sky.

'In my letters I have told you the story of Friday's dancing. But I have not told you the whole story.

'After Friday discovered your robes and wig and took them as his livery, he would spend entire days spinning and dancing and singing, after his fashion. What I did not tell you was that for his dancing he would wear nothing but the robes and wig. When he stood still he was covered to the ankles; but when he spun, the robes would stand out stiffly about him, so much so that one might have supposed the purpose of his dancing was to show forth the nakedness underneath.

'Now when Cruso told me that the slavers were in the habit of cutting out the tongues of their prisoners

118

to make them more tractable, I confess I wondered whether he might not be employing a figure, for the sake of delicacy: whether the lost tongue might stand not only for itself but for a more atrocious mutilation; whether by a dumb slave I was to understand a slave unmanned.

'When I heard the humming that first morning and came to the door and was met with the spectacle of Friday at his dancing with his robes flying about him, I was so confounded that I gaped without shame at what had hitherto been veiled from me. For though I had seen Friday naked before, it had been only from a distance: on our island we had observed the decencies as far as we could, Friday not least of us.

'I have told you of the abhorrence I felt when Cruso opened Friday's mouth to show me he had no tongue. What Cruso wanted me to see, what I averted my eyes from seeing, was the thick stub at the back of the mouth, which ever afterwards I pictured to myself wagging and straining under the sway of emotion as Friday tried to utter himself, like a worm cut in half contorting itself in death-throes. From that night on I had continually to fear that evidence of a yet more hideous mutilation might be thrust upon my sight.

'In the dance nothing was still and yet everything was still. The whirling robe was a scarlet bell settled upon Friday's shoulders and enclosing him; Friday was the dark pillar at its centre. What had been hidden from me was revealed. I saw; or, I should say, my eyes were open to what was present to them.

'I saw and believed I had seen, though afterwards I remembered Thomas, who also saw, but could not be brought to believe till he had put his hand in the wound.

'I do not know how these matters can be written of in a book unless they are covered up again in figures. When I first heard of you I was told you were a very secret man, a clergyman of sorts, who in the course of your work heard the darkest of confessions from the most desperate of penitents. I will not kneel before him like one of his gallows-birds, I vowed, with a mouth full of unspeakable confidences: I will say in plain terms what can be said and leave unsaid what cannot. Yet here I am pouring out my darkest secrets to you! You are like one of those notorious libertines whom women arm themselves against, but against whom they are at last powerless, his very notoriety being the seducer's shrewdest weapon.'

'You have not told me all I need to know of Bahia,' said Foe.

'I told myself (have I not confessed this before?): He is like the patient spider who sits at the heart of his web waiting for his prey to come to him. And when we struggle in his grasp, and he opens his jaws to devour us, and with our last breath we cry out, he smiles a thin smile and says: "I did not ask you to come visiting, you came of your own will."'

A long pause fell between us. 'Tossed on shores I never thought to visit' – the words came to me un-bidden. What was their meaning? From the street below came the noise of a woman scolding. On and on went her tirade. I smiled – I could not help myself – and Foe smiled too.

'As for Bahia,' I resumed, 'it is by choice that I say

so little of it. The story I desire to be known by is the story of the island. You call it an episode, but I call it a story in its own right. It commences with my being cast away there and concludes with the death of Cruso and the return of Friday and myself to England, full of new hope. Within this larger story are inset the stories of how I came to be marooned (told by myself to Cruso) and of Cruso's shipwreck and early years on the island (told by Cruso to myself), as well as the story of Friday, which is properly not a story but a puzzle or hole in the narrative (I picture it as a buttonhole, carefully cross-stitched around, but empty, waiting for the button). Taken in all, it is a narrative with a beginning and an end, and with pleasing digressions too, lacking only a substantial and varied middle, in the place where Cruso spent too much time tilling the terraces and I too much time tramping the shores. Once you proposed to supply a middle by inventing cannibals and pirates. These I would not accept because they were not the truth. Now you propose to reduce the island to an episode in the history of a woman in search of a lost daughter. This too I reject.

'You err most tellingly in failing to distinguish between my silences and the silences of a being such as Friday. Friday has no command of words and therefore no defence against being re-shaped day by day in conformity with the desires of others. I say he is a cannibal and he becomes a cannibal; I say he is a laundryman and he becomes a laundryman. What is the truth of Friday? You will respond: he is neither cannibal nor laundryman, these are mere names, they do not touch his essence, he is a substantial body, he is himself, Friday is Friday. But that is not so. No matter what he is to himself (is he anything to himself? – how can he tell us?), what he is to the world is what I make of him. Therefore the silence of Friday is a helpless silence. He is the child of his silence, a child unborn, a child waiting to be born that cannot be born. Whereas the silence I keep regarding Bahia and other matters is chosen and purposeful: it is my own silence. Bahia, I assert, is a world in itself, and Brazil an even greater world. Bahia and Brazil do not belong within an island story, they cannot be cramped into its confines. For instance: In the streets of Bahia you will see Negro women bearing trays of confections for sale. Let me name some few of these confections. There are *pamonhas* or Indian corn-cakes; *quimados*, made of sugar, called in French *bon-bons*; *pão de milho*, sponge-cake made with corn, and *pão de arroz*, made with rice; also *rolete de cana* or sugar-cane roll. These are the names that come to me; but there are many others, both sweet and savoury, and all to be found on a single confectioner's tray on the corner of any street. Think how much more there is of the strange and new in this vigorous city, where throngs of people surge through the streets day and night, naked Indians from the forests and ebony Dahomeyans and proud Lusitanians and half-breeds of every hue, where fat merchants are borne in litters by their slaves amid processions of flagellants and whirling dancers and food-vendors and crowds on their way to cock-fights. How can you ever close Bahia between the covers of a book? It is only small and thinly peopled places that can be subjugated and held down in words, such as desert islands and lonely houses. Besides, my daughter is no longer in Bahia but is gone into the interior, into a world so vast and strange I can hardly conceive it, a world of plains and plantations such as the one Cruso left behind, where the ant is emperor and everything is turned on its head.

'I am not, do you see, one of those thieves or highwaymen of yours who gabble a confession and are then whipped off to Tyburn and eternal silence, leaving you to make of their stories whatever you fancy. It is still in my power to guide and amend. Above all, to withhold. By such means do I still endeavour to be father to my story.'

Foe spoke. 'There is a story I would have you hear, Susan, from my days as visitor to Newgate. A woman, a convicted thief, as she was about to be led to the cart that would take her to Tyburn, asked for a minister to whom to make her true confession; for the confession she had made before, she said, was false. So the ordinary was summoned. To him she confessed again the thefts for which she had stood accused, and more besides; she confessed numerous impurities and blasphemies; she confessed to abandoning two children and stifling a third in the cot. She confessed a husband in Ireland and a husband transported to the Carolinas and a husband with her in Newgate, all alive. She detailed crimes of her young womanhood and crimes of her childhood, till at last, with the sun high in the heavens and the turnkey pounding at the door, the chaplain stilled her. "It is hard for me to believe, Mrs —," he said, "that a single lifetime can have sufficed for the commission of all these crimes. Are you truly as great a sinner as you would have me believe?" "If I do not speak the truth, reverend father," replied the woman (who was Irish, I may say), "then am I not abusing the sacrament, and is that not a sin worse even than those I have confessed, calling for further confession and repentance? And if my repentance is not truly felt (and is it truly felt? – I look into my heart and cannot say, so dark is it there), then is my confession not false, and is that not sin redoubled?" And the woman would have gone on confessing and throwing her confession in doubt all day long, till the carter dozed and the pie-men and the crowds went home, had not the chaplain held up his hands and in a loud voice shriven the woman, over all her protestations that her story was not done, and then hastened away.'

'Why do you tell me this story?' I asked. 'Am I the woman whose time has come to be taken to the gallows, and are you the chaplain?'

'You are free to give to the story what application you will,' Foe replied. 'To me the moral of the story is that there comes a time when we must give reckoning of ourselves to the world, and then forever after be content to hold our peace.'

'To me the moral is that he has the last word who disposes over the greatest force. I mean the executioner and his assistants, both great and small. If I were the Irishwoman, I should rest most uneasy in my grave knowing to what interpreter the story of my last hours has been consigned.'

'Then I will tell you a second story. A woman

124

(another woman) was condemned to die – I forget the crime. As the fatal day approached she grew more and more despairing, for she could find no one to take charge of her infant daughter, who was with her in the cell. At last one of her gaolers, taking pity on her distress, spoke with his wife, and together they agreed they would adopt the child as their own. When this condemned woman saw her child safe in the arms of her foster-mother, she turned to her captors and said: "Now you may do with me as you wish. For I have escaped your prison; all you have here is the husk of me" (intending, I believe, the husk that the butterfly leaves behind when it is born). This is a story from the old days; we no longer handle mothers so barbarously. Nevertheless, it retains its application, and the application is: There are more ways than one of living eternally.'

'Mr Foe, I do not have the skill of bringing out parables one after another like roses from a conjurer's sleeve. There was a time, I grant, when I hoped to be famous, to see heads turn in the street and hear folk whisper, "There goes Susan Barton the castaway." But that was an idle ambition, long since discarded. Look at me. For two days I have not eaten. My clothes are in tatters, my hair is lank. I look like an old woman, a filthy old gipsy-woman. I sleep in doorways, in churchyards, under bridges. Can you believe this beggar's life is what I desire? With a bath and new clothes and a letter of introduction from you I could tomorrow find myself a situation as a cook-maid, and a comfortable situation too, in a good house. I could return in every respect to the life of a substantial body,

[handwritten margin note: Thin hime she reminds us does not that she the power to have a]

the life you recommend. But such a life is abject. It is the life of a thing. A whore used by men is used as a substantial body. The waves picked me up and cast me ashore on an island, and a year later the same waves brought a ship to rescue me, and of the true story of that year, the story as it should be seen in God's great scheme of things, I remain as ignorant as a newborn babe. That is why I cannot rest, that is why I follow you to your hiding-place like a bad penny. Would I be here if I did not believe you to be my intended, the one alone intended to tell my true story?

'Do you know the story of the Muse, Mr Foe? The Muse is a woman, a goddess, who visits poets in the night and begets stories upon them. In the accounts they give afterwards, the poets say that she comes in the hour of their deepest despair and touches them with sacred fire, after which their pens, that have been dry, flow. When I wrote my memoir for you, and saw how like the island it was, under my pen, dull and vacant and without life, I wished that there were such a being as a man-Muse, a youthful god who visited authoresses in the night and made their pens flow. But now I know better. The Muse is both goddess and begetter. I was intended not to be the mother of my story, but to beget it. It is not I who am the intended, but you. But why need I argue my case? When is it ever asked of a man who comes courting that he plead in syllogisms? Why should it be demanded of me?'

Foe made no reply, but crossed the room to the curtained alcove and returned with a jar. 'These are wafers made with almond-paste after the Italian fashion,' he said. 'Alas, they are all I have to offer.'

I took one and tasted it. So light was it that it melted on my tongue. 'The food of gods,' I remarked. Foe smiled and shook his head. I held out a wafer to Friday, who languidly took it from my hand. 'The boy Jack will be coming shortly,' said Foe; 'then I will send him out for our supper.'

A silence fell. I gazed out at the steeples and roof-tops. 'You have found yourself a fine retreat,' I said – 'a true eagle's-nest. I wrote my memoir by candlelight in a windowless room, with the paper on my knee. Is that the reason, do you think, why my story was so dull – that my vision was blocked, that I could not see?'

'It is not a dull story, though it is too much the same,' said Foe.

'It is not dull so long as we remind ourselves it is true. But as an adventure it is very dull indeed. That is why you pressed me to bring in the cannibals, is it not?' Foe inclined his head judiciously this way and that. 'In Friday here you have a living cannibal,' I pursued. 'Behold. If we are to go by Friday, cannibals are no less dull than Englishmen.' 'They lose their vivacity when deprived of human flesh, I am sure,' replied Foe.

There was a tap at the door and the boy came in who had guided us to the house. 'Welcome, Jack!' called Foe. 'Mistress Barton, whom you have met, is to dine with us, so will you ask for double portions?' He took out his purse and gave Jack money. 'Do not forget Friday,' I put in. 'And a portion for Friday the manservant too, by all means,' said Foe. The boy departed. 'I found Jack among the waifs and orphans who sleep in the ash-pits at the glassworks. He is ten years old, by his reckoning, but already a notable pick-pocket.' 'Do you not try to correct him?' I inquired. 'To make him honest would be to condemn him to the work-house,' said Foe – 'Would you see a child in the work-house for the sake of a few handkerchiefs?' 'No; but you are training him for the gallows,' I replied – 'Can you not take him in and teach him his letters and send him out as an apprentice?' 'If I were to follow that advice, how many apprentices would I not have sleeping on my floor, whom I have saved from the streets?' said Foe – 'I should be taken for a thief-master and sent to the gallows myself. Jack has his own life to live, better than any I could devise for him.' 'Friday too has a life of his own,' I said; 'but I do not therefore turn Friday out on the streets.' 'Why do you not?' said Foe. 'Because he is helpless,' said I – 'Because London is strange to him. Because he would be taken for a runaway, and sold, and transported to Jamaica.' 'Might he not rather be taken in by his own kind, and cared for and fed?' said Foe – 'There are more Negroes in London than you would believe. Walk along Mile End Road on a summer's afternoon, or in Paddington, and you will see. Would Friday not be happier among other Negroes? He could play for pennies in a street band. There are many such strolling bands. I would make him a present of my flute.'

I glanced across at Friday. Did I mistake myself, or was there a gleam of understanding in his eye? 'Do you understand what Mr Foe says, Friday?' I called. He looked back at me dully.

'Or if we had mops in London, as they have in the west country,' said Foe, 'Friday could stand in the line with his hoe on his shoulder and be hired for a gardener, and not a word be passed.'

Jack now returned, bearing a covered tray from which came an appetizing smell. He set the tray down on the table and whispered to Foe. 'Allow us a few minutes, then show them up,' said Foe; and to me: 'We have visitors, but let us eat first.'

Jack had brought roast beef and gravy, together with a threepenny loaf and a pitcher of ale. There being only the two plates, Foe and I ate first, after which I filled my plate again and gave it to Friday.

There was a knock. Foe opened the door. The light fell on the girl I had left in Epping Forest; behind her in the shadows was another woman. While I yet stood dumbstruck the girl crossed the room and put her arms about me and kissed me on the cheek. A coldness went through me and I thought I would fall to the floor. 'And here is Amy,' said the girl – 'Amy, from Deptford, my nurse when I was little.' There was a pounding in my ears, but I made myself face Amy. I saw a slender, pleasant-faced woman of my age, with fair curls showing under her cap. 'I am happy to make your acquaintance,' I murmured; 'but I am sure I have never set eyes on you before in my life.'

Someone touched my arm. It was Foe: he led me to the chair and made me sit and gave me a glass of water. 'It is a passing dizziness,' I said. He nodded.

'So we are all together,' said Foe. 'Please be seated, Susan, Amy.' He indicated the bed. The boy Jack stood at Foe's side staring curiously at me. Foe lit a second lamp and set it on the mantel. 'In a moment Jack will fetch coals and make a fire for us, will you not, Jack?' 'Yes, sir,' said Jack.

I spoke. 'It is growing late, Friday and I will not be staying,' I said.

'You must not think of departing,' said Foe. 'You have nowhere to go; besides, when were you last in such company?'

'Never,' I replied. 'I was never before in such company in my life. I thought this was a lodging-house, but now I see it is a gathering-place for actors. It would be a waste of breath, Mr Foe, for me to say that these women are strangers to me, for you will only reply that I have forgotten, and then you will prompt them and they will embark on long stories of a past in which they will claim I was an actor too.

'What can I do but protest it is not true? I am as familiar as you with the many, many ways in which we can deceive ourselves. But how can we live if we do not believe we know who we are, and who we have been? If I were as obliging as you wish me to be – if I were ready to concede that, though I believe my daughter to have been swallowed up by the grasslands of Brazil, it is equally possible that she has spent the past year in England, and is here in this room now, in a form in which I fail to recognize her – for the daughter I remember is tall and dark-haired and has a name of her own – if I were like a bottle bobbing on the waves with a scrap of writing inside, that could as well be a message from an idle child fishing in the canal as from a mariner adrift on the high seas – if I were a mere receptacle ready to accommodate whatever story is stuffed in me, surely you would dismiss me, surely you would say to yourself, "This is no woman but a house of words, hollow, without substance"?

'I am not a story, Mr Foe. I may impress you as a story because I began my account of myself without preamble, slipping overboard into the water and striking out for the shore. But my life did not begin in the waves. There was a life before the water which stretched back to my desolate searchings in Brazil, thence to the years when my daughter was still with me, and so on back to the day I was born. All of which makes up a story I do not choose to tell. I choose not to tell it because to no one, not even to you, do I owe proof that I am a substantial being with a substantial history in the world. I choose rather to tell of the island, of myself and Cruso and Friday and what we three did there: for I am a free woman who asserts her freedom by telling her story according to her own desire.'

Here I paused, breathless. Both a girl and the woman Amy were watching me intently, I saw, and moreover with what seemed friendliness in their manner. Foe nodded as if to encourage me. The boy stood motionless with the coal-scuttle in his hand. Even Friday had his eyes on me.

I crossed the room. At my approach the girl, I observed, did not waver. What other test is left to me? I thought; and took her in my arms and kissed her on the lips, and felt her yield and kiss me in return, almost as one returns a lover's kiss. Had I expected her to dissolve when I touched her, her flesh crumbling and floating away like paper-ash? I gripped her tight and pressed my fingers into her shoulders. Was this truly my daughter's flesh? Opening my eyes, I saw Amy's face hovering only inches from mine, her lips parted too as if for a kiss. 'She is unlike me in every way,' I murmured. Amy shook her head. 'She is a true child of your womb,' she replied – 'She is like you in secret ways.' I drew back. 'I am not speaking of secret ways,' I said – 'I am speaking of blue eyes and brown hair'; and I might have made mention too of the soft and helpless little mouth, had I wished to be hurtful. 'She is her father's child as well as her mother's,' said Amy. To which I was about to reply that if the girl were her father's child then her father must be my opposite, and we do not marry our opposites, we marry men who are like us in subtle ways, when it struck me that I would likely be wasting my breath, for the light in Amy's eye was not so much friendly as foolish.

'Mr Foe,' I said, turning to him – and now I believe there was truly despair in my looks, and he saw it – 'I no longer know into what kind of household I have tumbled. I say to myself that this child, who calls herself by my name, is a ghost, a substantial ghost, if such beings exist, who haunts me for reasons I cannot understand, and brings other ghosts in tow. She stands for the daughter I lost in Bahia, I tell myself, and is sent by you to console me; but, lacking skill in summoning ghosts, you call up one who resembles my daughter in no respect whatever. Or you privately think my daughter is dead, and summon her ghost, and are allotted a ghost who by chance bears my name, with an attendant. Those are my surmises. As for the boy, I cannot tell whether he is a ghost or not, nor does it matter.

'But if these women are creatures of yours, visiting me at your instruction, speaking words you have prepared for them, then who am I and who indeed are you? I presented myself to you in words I knew to be my own – I slipped overboard, I began to swim, my hair floated about me, and so forth, you will remember the words – and for a long time afterwards, when I was writing those letters that were never read by you, and were later not sent, and at last not even written down, I continued to trust in my own authorship.

'Yet, in the same room as yourself at last, where I need surely not relate to you my every action – you have me under your eyes, you are not blind – I continue to describe and explain. Listen! I describe the dark staircase, the bare room, the curtained alcove, particulars a thousand times more familiar to you than to me; I tell of your looks and my looks, I relate your words and mine. Why do I speak, to whom do I speak, when there is no need to speak?

'In the beginning I thought I would tell you the story of the island and, being done with that, return to my former life. But now all my life grows to be story and there is nothing of my own left to me. I thought I was myself and this girl a creature from another order speaking words you made up for her. But now I am full of doubt. Nothing is left to me but doubt. I am doubt itself. Who is speaking me? Am I a phantom too? To what order do I belong? And you: who are you?'

Through all this talk Foe had stood stock still by the fireplace. I expected an answer, for never before had he failed for words. But instead, without preliminaries, he approached me and took me in his arms and kissed me; and, as the girl had responded before, I felt my lips answer his kiss (but to whom do I confess this?) as a woman's answer her lover's.

Was this his reply – that he and I were man and woman, that man and woman are beyond words? If so it was a paltry reply, demonstration more than reply, one that would satisfy no philosopher. Amy and the girl and Jack were smiling even broader than before. Breathless, I tugged myself free.

'Long ago, Mr Foe,' I said, 'you wrote down the story (I found it in your library and read it to Friday to pass the time) of a woman who spent an afternoon in conversation with a dear friend, and at the end of the afternoon embraced her friend and bade her farewell till they should next meet. But the friend, unknown to her, had died the day before, many miles away, and she had sat conversing with a ghost. Mrs Barfield was her name, you will remember. Thus I conclude you are aware that ghosts can converse with us, and embrace and kiss us too.'

'My sweet Susan,' said Foe – and I could not maintain my stern looks when he uttered these words, I had not been called sweet Susan for many years, certainly Cruso had never called me that – 'My sweet Susan, as to who among us is a ghost and who not I have nothing to say: it is a question we can only stare at in silence, like a bird before a snake, hoping it will not swallow us.

'But if you cannot rid yourself of your doubts, I have something to say that may be of comfort. Let us confront our worst fear, which is that we have all of us been called into the world from a different order (which we have now forgotten) by a conjurer unknown to us, as you say I have conjured up your daughter and her companion (I have not). Then I ask nevertheless: Have we thereby lost our freedom? Are you, for one, any less mistress of your life? Do we of necessity become puppets in a story whose end is invisible to us, and towards which we are marched like condemned felons? You and I know, in our different ways, how rambling an occupation writing is; and conjuring is surely much the same. We sit staring out of the window, and a cloud shaped like a camel passes by, and before we know it our fantasy has whisked us away to the sands of Africa and our hero (who is no one but ourselves in disguise) is clashing scimitars with a Moorish brigand. A new cloud floats past in the form of a sailing-ship, and in a trice we are cast ashore all woebegone on a desert isle. Have we cause to believe that the lives it is given us to live proceed with any more design than these whimsical adventures?

'You will say, I know, that the heroes and heroines of adventure are simple folk incapable of such doubts as those you feel regarding your own life. But have you considered that your doubts may be part of the story you live, of no greater weight than any other adventure of yours? I put the question merely.

'In a life of writing books, I have often, believe me, been lost in the maze of doubting. The trick I have learned is to plant a sign or marker in the ground where I stand, so that in my future wanderings I shall have something to return to, and not get worse lost than I am. Having planted it, I press on; the more often I come back to the mark (which is a sign to myself of my blindness and incapacity), the more certainly I know I am lost, yet the more I am heartened too, to have found my way back.

'Have you considered (and I will conclude here) that in your own wanderings you may, without knowing it, have left behind some such token for yourself; or, if you choose to believe you are not mistress of your life, that a token has been left behind on your behalf, which is the sign of blindness I have spoken of; and that, for lack of a better plan, your search for a way out of the maze – if you are indeed a-mazed or be-mazed – might start from that point and return to it as many times as are needed till you discover yourself to be saved?'

Here Foe turned from me to give his attention to Jack, who had for a while been tugging his sleeve. Low words passed between them; Foe gave him money; and, with a cheery Good-night, Jack took his leave. Then Mrs Amy looked at her watch and exclaimed at how late it was. 'Do you live far?' I asked her. She gave me a strange look. 'No,' she said, 'not far, not far at all.' The girl seemed reluctant to be off, but I embraced her again, and kissed her, which seemed to cheer her. Her appearances, or apparitions, or whatever they were, disturbed me less now that I knew her better.

'Come, Friday,' I said – 'it is time for us to go too.'

But Foe demurred. 'You will do me the greatest of

honours if you will spend the night here,' he said – 'Besides, where else will you find a bed?' 'So long as it does not rain we have a hundred beds to choose from, all of them hard,' I replied. 'Stay with me then,' said Foe – 'At the very least you shall have a soft bed.' 'And Friday?' 'Friday too,' said he. 'But where will Friday sleep?' 'Where would you have him sleep?' 'I will not send him away,' said I. 'By no means,' said he. 'May he sleep in your alcove then?' said I, indicating the corner of the room that was curtained off. 'Most certainly,' said he – 'I will lay down a mat, and a cushion too.' 'That will be enough,' said I.

While Foe made the alcove ready, I roused Friday. 'Come, we have a home for the night, Friday,' I whispered; 'and if fortune is with us we shall have another meal tomorrow.'

I showed him his sleeping-place and drew the curtain on him. Foe doused the light and I heard him undressing. I hesitated awhile, wondering what it augured for the writing of my story that I should grow so intimate with its author. I heard the bedsprings creak. 'Good night, Friday,' I whispered – 'Pay no attention to your mistress and Mr Foe, it is all for the good.' Then I undressed to my shift and let down my hair and crept under the bedclothes.

For a while we lay in silence, Foe on his side, I on mine. At last Foe spoke. 'I ask myself sometimes,' he said, 'how it would be if God's creatures had no need of sleep. If we spent all our lives awake, would we be better people for it or worse?'

To this strange opening I had no reply.

'Would we be better or worse, I mean,' he went on,

'if we were no longer to descend nightly into ourselves and meet what we meet there?'

'And what might that be?' said I.

'Our darker selves,' said he. 'Our darker selves, and other phantoms too.' And then, abruptly: 'Do you sleep, Susan?'

'I sleep very well, despite all,' I replied.

'And do you meet with phantoms in your sleep?'

'I dream, but I do not call the figures phantoms that come to me in dreams.'

'What are they then?'

'They are memories, memories of my waking hours, broken and mingled and altered.'

'And are they real?'

'As real, or as little real, as the memories themselves.'

'I read in an old Italian author of a man who visited, or dreamed he visited, Hell,' said Foe. 'There he met the souls of the dead. One of the souls was weeping. "Do not suppose, mortal," said this soul, addressing him, "that because I am not substantial these tears you behold are not the tears of a true grief."'

'True grief, certainly, but whose?' said I – 'The ghost's or the Italian's?' I reached out and took Foe's hand between mine. 'Mr Foe, do you truly know who I am? I came to you in the rain one day, when you were in a hurry to be off, and detained you with a story of an island which you could not have wished to hear.' ('You are quite wrong, my dear,' said Foe, embracing me.) 'You counselled me to write it down,' I went on, 'hoping perhaps to read of bloody doings on the high seas or the licentiousness of the Brazilians.'

('Not true, not true!' said Foe, laughing and hugging me – 'you roused my curiosity from the first, I was most eager to hear whatever you might relate!') 'But no, I pursue you with my own dull story, visiting it upon you now in your uttermost refuge. And I bring these women trailing after me, ghosts haunting a ghost, like fleas upon a flea. That is how it appears to you, does it not?' 'And why should you be, as you put it, haunting me, Susan?' 'For your blood. Is that not why ghosts return: to drink the blood of the living? Is that not the true reason why the shades made your Italian welcome?'

Instead of answering, Foe kissed me again, and in kissing gave such a sharp bite to my lip that I cried out and drew away. But he held me close and I felt him suck the wound. 'This is my manner of preying on the living,' he murmured.

Then he was upon me, and I might have thought myself in Cruso's arms again; for they were men of the same time of life, and heavy in the lower body, though neither was stout; and their way with a woman too was much the same. I closed my eyes, trying to find my way back to the island, to the wind and wave-roar; but no, the island was lost, cut off from me by a thousand leagues of watery waste.

I calmed Foe. 'Permit me,' I whispered – 'there is a privilege that comes with the first night, that I claim as mine.' So I coaxed him till he lay beneath me. Then I drew off my shift and straddled him (which he did not seem easy with, in a woman). 'This is the manner of the Muse when she visits her poets,' I whispered, and felt some of the listlessness go out of my limbs.

'A bracing ride,' said Foe afterwards – 'My very bones are jolted, I must catch my breath before we resume.' 'It is always a hard ride when the Muse pays her visits,' I replied – 'She must do whatever lies in her power to father her offspring.'

Foe lay still so long I thought he had gone to sleep. But just as I myself began to grow drowsy, he spoke: 'You wrote of your man Friday paddling his boat into the seaweed. Those great beds of seaweed are the home of a beast called by mariners the *kraken* – have you heard of it? – which has arms as thick as a man's thigh and many yards long, and a beak like an eagle's. I picture the kraken lying on the floor of the sea, staring up through tangled fronds of weeds at the sky, its many arms furled about it, waiting. It is into that terrible orbit that Friday steers his fragile craft.'

What led Foe to talk of sea-monsters at such a time I could not guess, but I held my peace.

'If a great arm had appeared and wrapped itself about Friday and without a sound drawn him beneath the waves, never to rise again, would it have surprised you?' he asked.

'A monstrous arm rising from the deep – yes, I would have been surprised. Surprised and unbelieving.'

'But surprised to see Friday disappear from the face of the waters, from the face of the earth?' Foe mused. Again he seemed to fall into a slumber. 'You say,' he said – and I woke up with a start – 'you say he was guiding his boat to the place where the ship went down, which we may surmise to have been a slave-ship, not a merchantman, as Cruso claimed. Well, then: picture the hundreds of his fellow-slaves – or their skeletons – still chained in the wreck, the gay little fish (that you spoke of) flitting through their eye-sockets and the hollow cases that had held their hearts. Picture Friday above, staring down upon them, casting buds and petals that float a brief while, then sink to settle among the bones of the dead.

'Does it not strike you, in these two accounts, how Friday is beckoned from the deep – beckoned or menaced, as the case may be? Yet Friday does not die. In his puny boat he floats upon the very skin of death and is safe.'

'It was not a boat but a log of wood,' said I.

'In every story there is a silence, some sight concealed, some word unspoken, I believe. Till we have spoken the unspoken we have not come to the heart of the story. I ask: Why was Friday drawn into such deadly peril, given that life on the island was without peril, and then saved?'

The question seemed fantastical. I had no answer.

'I said the heart of the story,' resumed Foe, 'but I should have said the eye, the eye of the story. Friday rows his log of wood across the dark pupil – or the dead socket – of an eye staring up at him from the floor of the sea. He rows across it and is safe. To us he leaves the task of descending into that eye. Otherwise, like him, we sail across the surface and come ashore none the wiser, and resume our old lives, and sleep without dreaming, like babes.'

'Or like a mouth,' said I. 'Friday sailed all unwitting across a great mouth, or beak as you called it, that stood open to devour him. It is for us to descend into the mouth (since we speak in figures). It is for us to open Friday's mouth and hear what it holds: silence, perhaps, or a roar, like the roar of a seashell held to the ear.'

'That too,' said Foe. 'I intended something else; but that too. We must make Friday's silence speak, as well as the silence surrounding Friday.'

'But who will do it?' I asked. 'It is easy enough to lie in bed and say what must be done, but who will dive into the wreck? On the island I told Cruso it should be Friday, with a rope about his middle for safety. But if Friday cannot tell us what he sees, is Friday in my story any more than a figuring (or pre-figuring) of another diver?'

Foe made no reply.

'All my efforts to bring Friday to speech, or to bring speech to Friday, have failed,' I said. 'He utters himself only in music and dancing, which are to speech as cries and shouts are to words. There are times when I ask myself whether in his earlier life he had the slight-est mastery of language, whether he knows what kind of thing language is.'

'Have you shown him writing?' said Foe.

'How can he write if he cannot speak? Letters are the mirror of words. Even when we seem to write in silence, our writing is the manifest of a speech spoken within ourselves or to ourselves.'

'Nevertheless, Friday has fingers. If he has fingers he can form letters. Writing is not doomed to be the shadow of speech. Be attentive to yourself as you write and you will mark there are times when the words form themselves on the paper *de novo*, as the Romans used to say, out of the deepest of inner silences. We are accustomed to believe that our world was created by God speaking the Word; but I ask, may it not rather be that he wrote it, wrote a Word so long we have yet to come to the end of it? May it not be that God continually writes the world, the world and all that is in it?'

'Whether writing is able to form itself out of nothing I am not competent to say,' I replied. 'Perhaps it will do so for authors; it will not for me. As to Friday, I ask nevertheless: How can he be taught to write if there are no words within him, in his heart, for writing to reflect, but on the contrary only a turmoil of feelings and urges? As to God's writing, my opinion is: If he writes, he employs a secret writing, which it is not given to us, who are part of that writing, to read.'

'We cannot read it, I agree, that was part of my meaning, since we are that which he writes. We, or some of us: it is possible that some of us are not written, but merely are; or else (I think principally of Friday) are written by another and darker author. Nevertheless, God's writing stands as an instance of a writing without speech. Speech is but a means through which the word may be uttered, it is not the word itself. Friday has no speech, but he has fingers, and those fingers shall be his means. Even if he had no fingers, even if the slavers had lopped them all off, he can hold a stick of charcoal between his toes, or between his teeth, like the beggars on the Strand. The waterskater, that is an insect and dumb, traces the name of God on the surfaces of ponds, or so the Arabians say. None is so deprived that he cannot write.'

Finding it as thankless to argue with Foe as it had been with Cruso, I held my tongue, and soon he fell asleep.

Whether the cause was the unfamiliar surroundings or Foe's body pressed against mine in the narrow bed I do not know; but, weary though I was, I could not sleep. Every hour I heard the watchman rapping on the doors below; I heard, or thought I heard, the patter of mouse-paws on the bare floor-boards. Foe began to snore. I endured the noise as long as I could; then I slipped out of bed and put on my shift and stood at the window staring over the starlit rooftops, wondering how long it was yet to the dawn. I crossed the room to Friday's alcove and drew aside the curtain. In the pitch blackness of that space was he asleep, or did he lie awake staring up at me? Again it struck me how lightly he breathed. One would have said he vanished when darkness fell, but for the smell of him, which I had once thought was the smell of woodsmoke, but now knew to be his own smell, drowsy and comfortable. A pang of longing went through me for the island. With a sigh I let the curtain drop and returned to bed. Foe's body seemed to grow as he slumbered: there was barely a handsbreadth of space left me. Let day come soon, I prayed; and in that instant fell asleep.

When I opened my eyes it was broad daylight and Foe was at his desk, with his back to me, writing. I dressed and crept over to the alcove. Friday lay on his mat swathed in his scarlet robes. 'Come, Friday,' I whispered – 'Mr Foe is at his labours, we must leave him.'

But before we reached the door, Foe recalled us. 'Have you not forgotten the writing, Susan?' he said. 'Have you not forgotten you are to teach Friday his letters?' He held out a child's slate and pencil. 'Come back at noon and let Friday demonstrate what he has learned. Take this for your breakfast.' And he gave me sixpence, which, though no great payment for a visit from the Muse, I accepted.

So we breakfasted well on new bread and milk, and then found a sunny seat in a churchyard. 'Do your best to follow, Friday,' I said – 'Nature did not intend me for a teacher, I lack patience.' On the slate I drew a house with a door and windows and a chimney, and beneath it wrote the letters h-o-u-s. 'This is the picture,' I said, pointing to the picture, 'and this the word.' I made the sounds of the word *house* one by one, pointing to the letters as I made them, and then took Friday's finger and guided it over the letters as I spoke the word; and finally gave the pencil into his hand and guided him to write h-o-u-s beneath the h-o-u-s I had written. Then I wiped the slate clean, so that there was no picture left save the picture in Friday's mind, and guided his hand in forming the word a third and a fourth time, till the slate was covered in letters. I wiped it clean again. 'Now do it alone, Friday,' I said; and Friday wrote the four letters h-o-u-s, or four shapes passably like them: whether they were truly the four letters, and stood truly for the word *house*, and the picture I had drawn, and the thing itself, only he knew.

I drew a ship in full sail, and made him write *ship*, and then began to teach him *Africa*. Africa I represented as a row of palm trees with a lion roaming among them. Was my Africa the Africa whose memory Friday bore within him? I doubted it. Nevertheless, I wrote A-f-r-i-c-a and guided him in forming the letters. So at the least he knew now that all words were not four letters long. Then I taught him m-o-th-e-r (a woman with a babe in arms), and, wiping the slate clean, commenced the task of rehearsing our four words. 'Ship,' I said, and motioned him to write. h-s-h-s-h-s he wrote, on and on, or perhaps h-f; and would have filled the whole slate had I not removed the pencil from his hand.

Long and hard I stared at him, till he lowered his eyelids and shut his eyes. Was it possible for anyone, however benighted by a lifetime of dumb servitude, to be as stupid as Friday seemed? Could it be that somewhere within him he was laughing at my efforts to bring him nearer to a state of speech? I reached out and took him by the chin and turned his face toward me. His eyelids opened. Somewhere in the deepest recesses of those black pupils was there a spark of mockery? I could not see it. But if it were there, would it not be an African spark, dark to my English eye? I sighed. 'Come, Friday,' I said, 'let us return to our master and show him how we have fared in our studies.'

It was midday. Foe was fresh-shaven and in good spirits.

'Friday will not learn,' I said. 'If there is a portal to his faculties, it is closed, or I cannot find it.'

'Do not be downcast,' said Foe. 'If you have planted a seed, that is progress enough, for the time being. Let us persevere: Friday may yet surprise us.'

'Writing does not grow within us like a cabbage while our thoughts are elsewhere,' I replied, not a little testily. 'It is a craft won by long practice, as you should know.'

Foe pursed his lips. 'Perhaps,' he said. 'But as there are many kinds of men, so there are many kinds of writing. Do not judge your pupil too hastily. He too may yet be visited by the Muse.'

While Foe and I spoke, Friday had settled himself on his mat with the slate. Glancing over his shoulder, I saw he was filling it with a design of, as it seemed, leaves and flowers. But when I came closer I saw the leaves were eyes, open eyes, each set upon a human foot: row upon row of eyes upon feet: walking eyes.

I reached out to take the slate, to show it to Foe, but Friday held tight to it. 'Give! Give me the slate, Friday!' I commanded. Whereupon, instead of obeying me, Friday put three fingers into his mouth and wet them with spittle and rubbed the slate clean.

I drew back in disgust. 'Mr Foe, I must have my freedom!' I cried. 'It is becoming more than I can bear! It is worse than the island! He is like the old man of the river!'

Foe tried to soothe me. 'The old man of the river,' he murmured – 'I believe I do not know whom you mean.'

'It is a story, nothing but a story,' I replied. 'There

was once a fellow who took pity on an old man waiting at the riverside, and offered to carry him across. Having borne him safely through the flood, he knelt to set him down on the other side. But the old man would not leave his shoulders: no, he tightened his knees about his deliverer's neck and beat him on his flanks and, to be short, turned him into a beast of burden. He took the very food from his mouth, and would have ridden him to his death had he not saved himself by a ruse.'

'I recognize the story now. It was one of the adventures of Sinbad of Persia.'

'So be it: I am Sinbad of Persia and Friday is the tyrant riding on my shoulders. I walk with him, I eat with him, he watches me while I sleep. If I cannot be free of him I will stifle!'

'Sweet Susan, do not fly into a passion. Though you say you are the ass and Friday the rider, you may be sure that if Friday had his tongue back he would claim the contrary. We deplore the barbarism of whoever maimed him, yet have we, his later masters, not reason to be secretly grateful? For as long as he is dumb we can tell ourselves his desires are dark to us, and continue to use him as we wish.'

'Friday's desires are not dark to me. He desires to be liberated, as I do too. Our desires are plain, his and mine. But how is Friday to recover his freedom, who has been a slave all his life? That is the true question. Should I liberate him into a world of wolves and expect to be commended for it? What liberation is it to be packed off to Jamaica, or turned out of doors into the night with a shilling in your hand? Even in his native Africa, dumb and friendless, would he know freedom? There is an urging that we feel, all of us, in our hearts, to be free; yet which of us can say what freedom truly is? When I am rid of Friday, will I then know freedom? Was Cruso free, that was despot of an island all his own? If so, it brought no joy to him that I could discover. As to Friday, how can Friday know what freedom means when he barely knows his name?'

'There is not need for us to know what freedom means, Susan. Freedom is a word like any word. It is a puff of air, seven letters on a slate. It is but the name we give to the desire you speak of, the desire to be free. What concerns us is the desire, not the name. Because we cannot say in words what an apple is, it is not forbidden us to eat the apple. It is enough that we know the names of our needs and are able to use these names to satisfy them, as we use coins to buy food when we are hungry. It is no great task to teach Friday such language as will serve his needs. We are not asked to turn Friday into a philosopher.'

'You speak as Cruso used to speak, Mr Foe, when he taught Friday *Fetch* and *Dig*. But as there are not two kinds of man, Englishman and savage, so the urgings of Friday's heart will not be answered by *Fetch* or *Dig* or *Apple*, or even by *Ship* and *Africa*. There will always be a voice in him to whisper doubts, whether in words or nameless sounds or tunes or tones.'

'If we devote ourselves to finding holes exactly shaped to house such great words as *Freedom*, H *onour*, *Bliss*, I agree, we shall spend a lifetime slipping and sliding and searching, and all in vain. They are words without a home, wanderers like the planets, and that is an end of it. But you must ask yourself, Susan: as it was a slaver's stratagem to rob Friday of his tongue, may it not be a slaver's stratagem to hold him in subjection while we cavil over words in a dispute we know to be endless?'

'Friday is no more in subjection than my shadow is for following me around. He is not free, but he is not in subjection. He is his own master, in law, and has been since Cruso's death.'

'Nevertheless, Friday follows you: you do not follow Friday. The words you have written and hung around his neck say he is set free; but who, looking at Friday, will believe them?'

'I am no slave-owner, Mr Foe. And before you think to yourself: Spoken like a true slave-owner!, should you not beware? As long as you close your ears to me, mistrusting every word I say as a word of slavery, poisoned, do you serve me any better than the slavers served Friday when they robbed him of his tongue?'

'I would not rob you of your tongue for anything, Susan. Leave Friday here for the afternoon. Go for a stroll. Take the air. See the sights. I am sadly enclosed. Be my spy. Come back and report to me how the world does.'

So I went for a stroll, and in the bustle of the streets began to recover my humour. I was wrong, I knew, to blame my state on Friday. If he was not a slave, was he nevertheless not the helpless captive of my desire to have our story told? How did he differ from one of the wild Indians whom explorers bring back with them, in a cargo of parakeets and golden idols and indigo and skins of panthers, to show they have truly been to the Americas? And might not Foe be a kind of captive too? I had thought him dilatory. But might the truth not be instead that he had laboured all these months to move a rock so heavy no man alive could budge it; that the pages I saw issuing from his pen were not idle tales of courtesans and grenadiers, as I supposed, but the same story over and over, in version after version, stillborn every time: the story of the island, as lifeless from his hand as from mine?

'Mr Foe,' I said, 'I have come to a resolution.'

But the man seated at the table was not Foe. It was Friday, with Foe's robes on his back and Foe's wig, filthy as a bird's nest, on his head. In his hand, poised over Foe's papers, he held a quill with a drop of black ink glistening at its tip. I gave a cry and sprang forward to snatch it away. But at that moment Foe spoke from the bed where he lay. 'Let him be, Susan,' he said in a tired voice: 'he is accustoming himself to his tools, it is part of learning to write.' 'He will foul your papers,' I cried. 'My papers are foul enough, he can make them no worse,' he replied – 'Come and sit with me.'

So I sat down beside Foe. In the cruel light of day I could not but mark the grubby sheets on which he lay, his long dirty fingernails, the heavy bags under his eyes.

'An old whore,' said Foe, as if reading my thoughts – 'An old whore who should ply her trade only in the dark.'

'Do not say that,' I protested. 'It is not whoring to entertain other people's stories and return them to the

world better dressed. If there were not authors to perform such an office, the world would be all the poorer.
Am I to damn you as a whore for welcoming me and
embracing me and receiving my story? You gave me a
home when I had none. I think of you as a mistress,
or even, if I dare speak the word, as a wife.'

'Before you declare yourself too freely, Susan, wait to
see what fruit I bear. But since we speak of childbearing,
has the time not come to tell me the truth about your
own child, the daughter lost in Bahia? Did you truly
give birth to her? Is she substantial or is she a story too?'

'I will answer, but not before you have told me: the
girl you send, the girl who calls herself by my name –
is she substantial?'

'You touch her; you embrace her; you kiss her.
Would you dare to say she is not substantial?'

'No, she is substantial, as my daughter is substantial
and I am substantial; and you too are substantial, no
less and no more than any of us. We are all alive, we
are all substantial, we are all in the same world.'

'You have omitted Friday.'

I turned back to Friday, still busy at his writing.
The paper before him was heavily smudged, as by a
child unused to the pen, but there was writing on it,
writing of a kind, rows and rows of the letter *o* tightly
packed together. A second page lay at his elbow, fully
written over, and it was the same.

'Is Friday learning to write?' asked Foe.

'He is writing, after a fashion,' I said. 'He is writing
the letter *o*.'

'It is a beginning,' said Foe. 'Tomorrow you must
teach him *a*.'

IV

The staircase is dark and mean. On the landing I stumble over a body. It does not stir, it makes no sound. By the light of a match I make out a woman or a girl, her feet drawn up inside a long grey dress, her hands folded under her armpits; or is it that her limbs are unnaturally short, the stunted limbs of a cripple? Her face is wrapped in a grey woollen scarf. I begin to unwrap it, but the scarf is endless. Her head lolls. She weighs no more than a sack of straw.

The door is not locked. Through a solitary window moonlight floods the room. There is a quick scurrying across the floor, a mouse or a rat.

They lie side by side in bed, not touching. The skin, dry as paper, is stretched tight over their bones. Their lips have receded, uncovering their teeth, so that they seem to be smiling. Their eyes are closed.

I draw the covers back, holding my breath, expecting disturbance, dust, decay; but they are quietly composed, he in a nightshirt, she in her shift. There is even a faint smell of lilac.

At the first tug the curtain across the alcove tears. The corner is in pitch darkness, and in the air of this room my matches will not strike. Kneeling, groping, I find the man Friday stretched at full length on his back. I touch his feet, which are hard as wood, then feel my way up the soft, heavy stuff in which his body is wrapped, to his face.

Though his skin is warm, I must search here and there before I find the pulse in his throat. It is faint, as if his heart beat in a far-off place. I tug lightly at his hair. It is indeed like lambswool.

His teeth are clenched. I press a fingernail between the upper and lower rows, trying to part them.

Face down I lie on the floor beside him, the smell of old dust in my nostrils.

After a long while, so long I might even have been asleep, he stirs and sighs and turns on to his side. The sound his body makes is faint and dry, like leaves falling over leaves. I raise a hand to his face. His teeth part. I press closer, and with an ear to his mouth lie waiting.

At first there is nothing. Then, if I can ignore the beating of my own heart, I begin to hear the faintest faraway roar: as she said, the roar of waves in a seashell; and over that, as if once or twice a violin-string were touched, the whine of the wind and the cry of a bird.

Closer I press, listening for other sounds: the chirp of sparrows, the thud of a mattock, the call of a voice.

From his mouth, without a breath, issue the sounds of the island.

*   *

At one corner of the house, above head-height, a plaque is bolted to the wall. *Daniel Defoe*, *Author*, are the words, white on blue, and then more writing too small to read.

I enter. Though it is a bright autumn day, light does not penetrate these walls. On the landing I stumble over the body, light as straw, of a woman or a girl. The room is darker than before; but, groping along the mantel, I find the stub of a candle and light it. It burns with a dull blue flame.

The couple in the bed lie face to face, her head in the crook of his arm.

Friday, in his alcove, has turned to the wall. About his neck – I had not observed this before – is a scar like a necklace, left by a rope or chain.

The table is bare save for two dusty plates and a pitcher. On the floor is a dispatch box with brass hinges and clasp. I lift it on to the table and open it. The yellowed topmost leaf crumbles in a neat half-moon under my thumb. Bringing the candle nearer, I read the first words of the tall, looping script: 'Dear Mr Foe, At last I could row no further.'

With a sigh, making barely a splash, I slip overboard. Gripped by the current, the boat bobs away, drawn south toward the realm of the whales and eternal ice. Around me on the waters are the petals cast by Friday.

I strike out toward the dark cliffs of the island; but something dull and heavy gropes at my leg, something caresses my arm. I am in the great bed of seaweed: the fronds rise and fall with the swell.

With a sigh, with barely a splash, I duck my head

under the water. Hauling myself hand over hand down the trunks, I descend, petals floating around me like a rain of snowflakes.

The dark mass of the wreck is flecked here and there with white. It is huge, greater than the leviathan: a hulk shorn of masts, split across the middle, banked on all sides with sand. The timbers are black, the hole even blacker that gives entry. If the kraken lurks anywhere, it lurks here, watching out of its stony hooded undersea eyes.

Sand rises in slow flurries around my feet. There are no swarms of gay little fish. I enter the hole.

I am below deck, the port side of the ship beneath my feet, feeling my way along beams and struts soggy to the touch. The stub of candle hangs on a string around my neck. I hold it up before me like a talisman, though it sheds no light.

Something soft obstructs me, perhaps a shark, a dead shark overgrown with pulpy flowers of the sea, or the body of a guardian wrapped in rotting fabric, turn after turn. On hands and knees I creep past it.

I had not thought the sea could be dirty. But the sand under my hands is soft, dank, slimy, outside the circulation of the waters. It is like the mud of Flanders, in which generations of grenadiers now lie dead, trampled in the postures of sleep. If I am still for more than a moment I begin to sink, inch by inch.

I come to a bulkhead and a stairway. The door at the head of the stairway is closed; but when I put a shoulder to it and push, the wall of water yields and I can enter.

It is not a country bath-house. In the black space of

this cabin the water is still and dead, the same water as yesterday, as last year, as three hundred years ago. Susan Barton and her dead captain, fat as pigs in their white nightclothes, their limbs extending stiffly from their trunks, their hands, puckered from long immersion, held out in blessing, float like stars against the low roof. I crawl beneath them.

In the last corner, under the transoms, half buried in sand, his knees drawn up, his hands between his thighs, I come to Friday.

I tug his woolly hair, finger the chain about his throat. 'Friday,' I say, I try to say, kneeling over him, sinking hands and knees into the ooze, 'what is this ship?'

But this is not a place of words. Each syllable, as it comes out, is caught and filled with water and diffused. This is a place where bodies are their own signs. It is the home of Friday.

He turns and turns till he lies at full length, his face to my face. The skin is tight across his bones, his lips are drawn back. I pass a fingernail across his teeth, trying to find a way in.

His mouth opens. From inside him comes a slow stream, without breath, without interruption. It flows up through his body and out upon me; it passes through the cabin, through the wreck; washing the cliffs and shores of the island, it runs northward and southward to the ends of the earth. Soft and cold, dark and unending, it beats against my eyelids, against the skin of my face.

READ MORE IN PENGUIN

In every corner of the world, on every subject under the sun, Penguin represents quality and variety – the very best in publishing today.

For complete information about books available from Penguin – including Puffins, Penguin Classics and Arkana – and how to order them, write to us at the appropriate address below. Please note that for copyright reasons the selection of books varies from country to country.

In the United Kingdom: Please write to *Dept. JC, Penguin Books Ltd, FREEPOST, West Drayton, Middlesex UB7 OBR*

If you have any difficulty in obtaining a title, please send your order with the correct money, plus ten per cent for postage and packaging, to *PO Box No. 11, West Drayton, Middlesex UB7 OBR*

In the United States: Please write to *Penguin USA Inc., 375 Hudson Street, New York, NY 10014*

In Canada: Please write to *Penguin Books Canada Ltd, 10 Alcorn Avenue, Suite 300, Toronto, Ontario M4V 3B2*

In Australia: Please write to *Penguin Books Australia Ltd, 487 Maroondah Highway, Ringwood, Victoria 3134*

In New Zealand: Please write to *Penguin Books (NZ) Ltd,182–190 Wairau Road, Private Bag, Takapuna, Auckland 9*

In India: Please write to *Penguin Books India Pvt Ltd, 706 Eros Apartments, 56 Nehru Place, New Delhi 110 019*

In the Netherlands: Please write to *Penguin Books Netherlands B.V., Keizersgracht 231 NL–1016 DV Amsterdam*

In Germany: Please write to *Penguin Books Deutschland GmbH, Friedrichstrasse 10–12, W–6000 Frankfurt/Main 1*

In Spain: Please write to *Penguin Books S. A., C. San Bernardo 117–6° E–28015 Madrid*

In Italy: Please write to *Penguin Italia s.r.l., Via Felice Casati 20, I–20124 Milano*

In France: Please write to *Penguin France S. A., 17 rue Lejeune, F–31000 Toulouse*

In Japan: Please write to *Penguin Books Japan, Ishikiribashi Building, 2–5–4, Suido, Tokyo 112*

In Greece: Please write to *Penguin Hellas Ltd, Dimocritou 3, GR–106 71 Athens*

In South Africa: Please write to *Longman Penguin Southern Africa (Pty) Ltd, Private Bag X08, Bertsham 2013*

BY THE SAME AUTHOR

Age of Iron

Winner of the 1990 Sunday Express *Book of the Year Award*

'Elizabeth Curren has cancer ... As if on cue, a derelict alcoholic sets up camp beside her house, waiting for her demise ... He is Vercueil, the angel of death, a man who becomes the Virgil to Elizabeth's Dante ...' – James Runcie in the *Daily Telegraph*. 'Wholly and magnificently original' – Francis King in the *Spectator*

Life and Times of Michael K

Winner of the 1983 Booker Prize

Michael K, blemished by a harelip and made redundant from his job, chooses to ignore the civil war raging around him and takes his ailing mother out of Cape Town back to the farm of her childhood. His mother dies on the journey and he is twice imprisoned. 'Coetzee's ... writing gives off whiffs of Conrad, of Nabokov, of Golding, of the Paul Theroux of *The Mosquito Coast*' – Victoria Glendinning

Dusklands

A specialist in psychological warfare and a megalomaniac Boer. Together these men represent a paradox of chilling extremes – for as they push back the frontiers of knowledge, so too they assist at the death of the spirit. 'J. M. Coetzee's vision goes to the nerve-centre of being. What he finds there is more than most people will ever know about themselves' – Nadine Gordimer

In the Heart of the Country

The impassioned diary of a young woman living on a remote farm in South Africa, *In the Heart of the Country* is a portrait of loneliness, festering anger and inevitable madness conveyed with tremendous power and certainty. 'A remarkable piece of sustained intensity ... a tour de force' – *Daily Telegraph*

also published

Waiting for the Barbarians